JAGGED WAVES

Jillian Night

THIS INSPIRING NOVEL CAN TAKE YOU BACK TO
YOUR YOUTH AND INSTILL A DESIRE TO LIVE
LIFE TO THE FULLEST NO MATTER THE AGE
ON YOUR DRIVER'S LICENSE.

Jillian

JAGGED
WAVES

PROLOGUE

Is it possible? Meredith wondered as she stared at the tall, handsome man walking through the terrace doors towards her. She was so startled she had to reach for the back of a chair to steady herself. Thank heavens the wine in her glass was white. It would be quite embarrassing to spill red wine on this glorious carpet.

It had been forty years since she had seen his face. Their parting had been bittersweet but also the absolute right thing to do. After all, they were married to and had children with other people. If their affair had progressed that evening on the Phoenix riverbank she and Paul Richardson thought of as their private place, so many lives would have been ruined.

"Excuse me," he said. "I know this is an old, well-used line, but don't I know you? Aren't you Meredith Jamison?" Paul continued as he reached for her hand.

"Actually, it is Meredith Jamison Evans, and yes, you definitely know me, Paul Richardson. I can't believe it is really you!" Meredith exclaimed. "What a surprise to see you again, especially at a Washington, DC, State Department gathering.," she said as she smiled and shook his hand warmly.

"Do you live in Washington, Meredith?" Paul asked hopefully.

"No, I live in San Diego on Coronado Island. I am

here for a few days visiting a dear friend, Karen Hall. She invited me to be her guest this evening but is running a bit late. And you—do you live in Washington, Paul?"

"I do," he responded.

Just as he began to ask his next question, Karen came rushing towards them spilling over with apologies for being late. She realized immediately she had interrupted something but was not sure just what. Meredith released Paul's hand and said, "Karen, this is Paul Richardson, an old friend from Phoenix I haven't seen in years."

To Meredith's surprise, Karen smiled, reached for Paul's extended hand, said, "Great to see you again Paul," and then she excused herself in search of a stiff drink. Meredith glanced between her two friends in astonishment as Karen walked away.

Just then the guests were called to dinner. "We must continue this conversation very soon," Paul said as he offered her his arm to lead them towards the dining room.

CHAPTER 1

Meredith sat staring at the beautiful Pacific Ocean she loved. As her eyes followed the waves towards the shore, her head naturally turned to the man sitting beside her. She loved him more than life itself. Alex Evans still thrilled her after forty years of marriage.

He was no longer a lanky sailor in his Navy whites but a real man's man, all six feet four, two hundred and thirty pounds of him. She smiled, thinking how happy she was when he finally grew into his ears, as they had always seemed too big for his head.

She adjusted the high back on her yellow beach chair and was almost asleep when Alex announced, "Sweetheart, I am due at the golf course in a few minutes, just a quick nine holes with the boys. I'll be back in a couple of hours." He stood up, leaned over, and held her face in his large hands as he gave her a loving goodbye kiss.

Meredith grinned up at him. "I'll have the cocktails ready when you get home." She watched him stride away through the sand and settled back in her chair.

Sometime later, still lying in her beach chair she stirred and realized she had fallen asleep and dreamed of the wonderful life she and Alex had enjoyed. But it was cocktail time and she quickly pulled herself together, packed up her beach bag, and headed upstairs.

She got busy setting out the gin and tonic, sure Alex would return any moment. Then the telephone rang, and her life changed forever.

The call was not from Alex, but from Tom, his closest friend. As soon as Meredith answered, Tom blurted, "Meredith, we were saying goodbye on the 9th green when Alex collapsed. No warning or anything, he just dropped. I did CPR until the paramedics got here, just a minute ago. They're taking him to Sharp Coronado emergency, but Meredith—he's not conscious. I'll meet you there."

Tears poured down her face, and her heart actually hurt as she gasped for breath. Before shock could overwhelm her, she grabbed her purse, took the elevator down to the garage, and raced to the small hospital located at the other end of the island.

Tom met her at the entrance to the emergency room. "They're working on him and won't let us in back, but they said someone will come out to tell us what's happening."

Just a few minutes later, the ER doctor came out and regretfully told them Alex couldn't be saved. He'd died instantly, apparently of a massive brain aneurysm. The doctor took her back to say goodbye to Alex, and her world as she knew it collapsed.

The celebration of life a week later was as Alex would have wanted, held at the nearby Coronado Golf

Club where he played so often for many years. All his golfing buddies were in attendance and deeply saddened by the loss of their dear friend.

Alex had been a devoted husband and their three grown children each offered heartfelt eulogies for the father they had adored. She sat surrounded by her children and grandchildren feeling almost regal. The queen of a kingdom of one.

The condolences shared by their well-meaning friends, all reminders of times they had spent with Alex, quickly became too heavy for Meredith to bear. She wanted to scream. The urge to run was so great she pulled Stephen aside, and tearfully begged, "Please take me home. I know the girls can take over for me. I'll see them later at the condo after all this is over."

Meredith was quiet on the drive back to the beach. Stephen sat behind the wheel of the Lincoln Navigator; a job always delegated to his father. No cheers from Alex's favorite baseball team, the San Diego Padres, came through the radio. Just silence. But then, death was silent, so silent. She didn't want to go home but didn't know where else to go.

It was all so tragic and Meredith could not yet begin to imagine her life without him. Loyal to her for over forty years, Alex had promised he would never leave her. It was the one promise in all their years together he was not able to keep.

Stephen drove into the Shores complex, passing from one gate to another and into the darkness of the underground parking structure which seemed to engulf them as they entered. Their designated parking spot stood empty as if waiting for the loving couple who resided there.

They entered the building and the doorman bowed his head and made a sign of the cross. Meredith nodded in acknowledgment of his thoughtfulness. He activated the elevator and reminded them to *push the button.* As the elevator doors opened, she entered, clutching the ring of keys she always carried.

Their corner apartment was on the seventh floor of the sixteen-story building. Stephen took her arm and could feel her lean into him for support. "Are you all right, Mother?" he asked, but she only nodded in response.

Meredith walked across the room to the windows. She stood frozen, staring out at the beach below. "How could he leave me?" she said in a whisper.

Soon it would be a night she had dreaded all her married life. They had traveled apart over the years, but this was a different journey. This time there would be no calls to say good night, and she would forever open the door to find no one at home.

She stood at the window watching the jagged waves and thinking about the comings and goings of the ocean tide. As tears streamed down her cheeks much like those salty waves, she couldn't begin to fathom what life held in store for her.

CHAPTER 2

In the months following Alex's death, Meredith felt she was walking through a haze. She found little reason to cook and forced herself to accept a few invitations from well-meaning friends trying to keep her busy. Everything was an effort, even just getting out of bed each morning. She found herself lying down in the middle of the afternoon, napping in her darkened bedroom. She had gone from being a vital part of a couple to a lonely single woman.

Meredith tried to establish some order in her life. She reorganized their apartment, working to make it more hers, but Alex kept showing up. His favorite pair of golf shoes still stood beside his golf clubs in the hall closet. She could not bring herself to take that final step and give away one of her last connections to him when seeing them always brought back wonderful memories of their life together.

Everyone told them they lived a charmed life and were the perfect couple. Looking back, she had to agree.

Suddenly immersed in recollections of how they had met on a blind date, Meredith remembered thinking —

— what in the world do I have in common with a San Diego-based sailor on weekend leave, even if he is Dad's secretary's son? I hope my father remembers asking me for this favor.

When a loud car pulled up in front of my parents' home I stole a quick peek at the tall, rangy stranger walking up the front steps. He sported a big, wide smile, his hair combed back in an Elvis pompadour, and he was wearing the gaudiest gold lamé western shirt I had ever seen.

This date had disaster written all over it!

When the night ended with a stiff handshake at my front door, I hoped it was the last I would ever see of Alex Evans, whether he had a great smile or not.

A week later he was back in town and asked me out again. I tried to interest him in one of my sorority sisters, but he insisted I was the one he wanted to see and somehow convinced me to agree to a date at the movies.

I remember sitting next to him in the darkened theater and being so aware of his warmth, size, and deep infectious laugh. My hands stayed clutched in my lap, and I sat stiff as a board, trying hard to ignore him, but it was impossible. Even though he was only a year older than my nineteen years, Alex wasn't a boy; he was a man.

At the end of the evening, I had mixed feelings as he hadn't even tried to hold my hand or kiss me goodnight, something I was quick to remind him of on our honeymoon.

When I didn't hear from him for a couple of

weeks, I thought he must have read all my negative signals and moved on. Why did I feel so disappointed? Why did I keep thinking about his smile, his blue eyes?

When he called two weeks later he explained his ship had been deployed on maneuvers. Could I forgive him for not calling, and see him again the following weekend?

That Friday I waited. And waited. Long after my parents went to bed, I fell asleep on the couch still hoping he might show up. When Alex tapped on the window about midnight, I looked out, right into the deep blue eyes of a tall man wearing his Navy dress whites. *That was all it took.*

I opened the front door and he swept me into his arms for our first kiss. From the look in his eyes and the wild beating of my heart, I knew it wouldn't be our last.

Our world soon revolved around his weekend visits and loving times spent together at the river bank. We wanted to marry but there was so little time before his deployment in December. Alex proudly asked my father for my hand in marriage and he happily approved. His family was another story. His mother saw a distinct class difference and objected bitterly to the marriage.

Alex and I overruled her and plans were made for a small church wedding. I walked down the aisle in a wedding dress borrowed from one of my sorority sisters and Alex wore the only suit he owned. It was blue with sleeves too short for his still growing arms, but nothing mattered except our young love.

Our brief honeymoon was one night in the glamorous Motel 6 on the street above Pier One in San Diego, where his ship stood ready to sail to Japan in the early morning hours.

Could we cram seven months of lovemaking into twenty-four hours? We would sure give it a try! Protection was the least of our worries as we experienced intimacy as husband and wife, and sex became enduring love in that tacky hotel room we laughed about for many years. Our hands roamed over one another as if trying to memorize each other's bodies before our time apart, and we made love throughout the entire night.

For that wonderful night, we had each other and Johnny Mathis crooning on the radio. The next morning when it was time to ship out, we held tight to each other and both cried.

I settled into married life in my parents' home still sleeping in my childhood bed and working part-time at the drug store. By February I knew I was pregnant. Would Alex want a child so soon in our marriage? Correspondence was only by mail in those days and could take up to two weeks. Alex quickly responded he was surprised and very excited.

The heat in Phoenix was brutal that summer and the doctor gave his approval for me to travel, so off I went with my parents to our family vacation spot, San Diego's Mission Bay. I spent the days playing cards, walking on the beach dreaming of Alex, and silently hoping someday this wonderful city could be our home.

While I dreamed, the small child inside me had

other ideas and decided to enter the world on his terms. I woke my parents and together we three out-of-towners went searching for the nearest hospital. Within hours, a tiny baby boy was placed in my arms.

A few days later my parents went down to Pier One to meet the USS Piedmont and bring Alex to our first home, a small one-bedroom apartment in Pacific Beach. When he arrived, I took his hand and led him to meet Stephen, our new son. Alex's eyes filled with tears of love for his child and his child-like bride standing beside him.

As Meredith relived her earliest years with Alex, she sent a prayer of gratitude to her father who had asked her for the favor that changed her life.

CHAPTER 3

Alex finished his tour with the Navy in 1961 and the family moved into a small apartment in Phoenix. Within a year daughter, Jennifer was born.

Taking advantage of his Navy benefits and training, he enrolled at Arizona State University in its relatively new engineering program. After graduation in '65, he quickly put his new degree to work with a company responsible for the expansion of roads and freeways through the rapidly growing city and used that as the stepping-stone to other major projects throughout the Southwest. As his work responsibilities grew so did their family with a second daughter, Claire.

Alex soon found himself on the road too often and after almost being killed in a tornado, he and Meredith took that as the sign they had been watching for. Their dinner conversations frequently included discussions of a desire to relocate to a smaller city and chose the desert community of Palm Springs, California.

He found an engineering position with the City of Palm Springs and was able to continue the work he enjoyed while remaining full-time with the family he loved. After a few years, he had established an excellent reputation in their new community and decided to venture out with his own engineering firm. He opened an office in Palm Desert and used his background on a new venture—building golf courses—the number one activity in the desert. He worked with many famous golf course celebrities and designers and became a builder for the *stars of golf.*

Meredith settled nicely in their new city. While shopping one day, she was delighted when she ran into her old friend Stacy from their college days in Phoenix. Stacy, the sorority sister who had loaned Meredith her wedding dress, also lived in Palm Springs with her family.

Meredith always wanted to own a small business—to be an entrepreneur. When they reconnected, she decided it was time. She and Stacy became partners in *The Silver Pear*, where they proudly sold everything for the kitchen to the top of the table. Their flagship store was soon so successful it became the number one location for the wealthy clientele of Palm Springs, and their interior designers, to come and outfit the mansions they called home. A couple of years after their initial grand opening Meredith and Stacy added a second location in Palm Desert.

Unfortunately, Stacy's marriage was not as successful as her business partnership with Meredith. After Stacy divorced, she sold her share of the business to Meredith and left Palm Springs for the mountains of Idaho.

Nine years after opening his golf course business in the desert, Alex's reputation with golf course development extended to Las Vegas, another city where golf was king. He was approached by a pro golfer to construct a new golf course that could launch the pro as a developer of his own signature courses. Alex and Meredith debated whether he should take the contract but eventually decided it was an offer he couldn't refuse. The only problem would be his need to spend a great deal of time away from Meredith, and although she was busy with her retail world, both knew starting a new project would take time and energy away from their life together.

One night while lying cuddled in his massive arms, Meredith offered a proposal. "Let's open another Silver Pear in Summerlin. After all, there are kitchens, dining rooms, and high-end clients in Las Vegas also."

Although he wasn't surprised by her suggestion, Alex asked, "How would you manage a new store in addition to the two in the desert?"

Meredith had the answer ready for him. "Jennifer can take over those stores." Their oldest daughter had joined the staff years before, first as the store's bookkeeper and now as second in command, thanks to her excellent business savvy.

Meredith got her wish and within weeks they were in Vegas scouting locations for new office space for him and a prime retail spot for her. They would be even busier than in California but knew they were still young enough to establish the new ventures and also enjoy the exciting opportunities life in Vegas could offer. It seemed a perfect solution, providing a base for family and friends who wanted to visit the Strip and yet close enough to the desert so Jen and

Meredith could travel to national markets together to purchase goods for all three stores.

The move proved to be a wonderful time in all of their lives until that fateful day when Meredith got the call from a neighbor telling her there appeared to be something terribly wrong at their home. It was a day she would never forget.

Alex and Meredith had settled into a beautiful home decorated in soft white and taupe tones, with stone pillars, and perfectly placed furniture. It was the envy of the few friends and neighbors they shared in the up-scale, gated Las Vegas community. They were happy in the house, but three years later put it on the market when they found the perfect location for the retirement home of their dreams on a hilltop with amazing views of the Strip.

Rushing home after receiving the distressed call from a neighbor, they opened the doors to find the floors littered with dirt, drawers open and dumped, cabinets flung open, and loose wires hanging everywhere. Stunned by the destruction in front of them, Alex immediately phoned the police.

"911 — what's your emergency?"

"We've been robbed! Send someone now! Our home is ransacked ... anything they didn't take, they threw on the floor."

"Okay, sir, what is your address?"

Once Alex provided that information, the dispatcher continued, "Please wait outside your home for the patrol car to arrive in case there is someone still inside."

"It's obvious they're gone, but we will wait in the front yard. It's almost too heartbreaking to be inside. Please hurry."

To quote the police, the burglars were professionals, and the Evans home had been cased by a couple posing as prospective buyers. The realtor who brought the couple to view the home admitted she picked them up at the Paris Hotel as a cold call. Ten days after the viewing they returned, broke through a side garage door, and backed a truck inside. Once out of sight, they took their time loading the stolen treasures. When they finished, the burglars opened the garage door and simply drove away, leaving a trail of black wires crawling out from under the closing garage door.

When the police left, leaving behind the additional insult of fingerprint powder, Meredith and Alex began cleaning up their ransacked home. They worked together as they had for thirty-five years, silent, each suffering in their own way. Floors were vacuumed, closets that had been roughly pawed through by strangers were straightened, and personal items were folded and put back in place.

Meredith wondered how she could ever feel comfortable again in their large spacious bedroom without seeing her private and personal belongings strewn about the room. That was all she could think about as she lay cradled in his strong arms until nearly three a.m. when she finally drifted into a restless sleep.

No longer able to feel secure in the house and at their family's insistence, the couple admitted their time in Las Vegas was over. The construction of the dream home on top of a hill was canceled, their businesses sold, and they returned to the desert.

Retirement was still approaching, but now discouraged by their losses in Las Vegas, they questioned where their dream home might be found. Maybe the beach they loved? So back to San Diego, they went, where their story had begun.

During one of their house-hunting trips, they took time to visit a dear friend, Bill Hamilton. He lived in a beautiful condo in one of the many tall towers of The Shores community on Coronado Island. Located on the beach, it provided all the amenities she and Alex felt they would ever need, so they decided to speak with one of the on-site realtors. They spent most of the afternoon visiting various units and knew which one was *theirs* as soon as the realtor opened the door. The condo was only available for lease, but that worked into Alex's and Meredith's plans perfectly, allowing them to maintain their Palm Springs home while escaping to the beach on weekends. Once they retired, they would sell their desert home and move permanently to Coronado.

By the time of his retirement, Alex had worked on over seventy golf courses in the ever-growing desert communities. Meredith had become the entrepreneur she dreamed of being, opening three Silver Pear locations in two states, and after twenty-nine years was able to turn a thriving, successful business over to Jennifer. And the condo they had been leasing for several years was unexpectedly offered to them for purchase.

Her memories both soothed and saddened her. She forced herself to walk the beach they had strolled together for so many years and tried to remember happier times. The yellow beach chairs favored by her family seemed everywhere on the sand but she knew that was merely a mirage. Theirs were locked away in the storage with the rest of the beach paraphernalia she and Alex had shared.

She now sat in her new blue beach chair, watching the current season of beachgoers. The young boys surfing, the small children building their sandcastles, the girls in their bikinis who were beginning to look younger every day, and the Navy pilots practicing their touch and goes.

The condominium buildings of the Shores are located on the Silver Strand, near the Naval Air Station in Coronado and the loud approach of the jet planes practicing their maneuvers always made her look skyward. Alex had loved the sound of their roaring engines; now the sounds saddened her.

She often recalled September 11, 2001, when the beautiful blue skies of Coronado were eerie and quiet. No planes flew, no one sat on the beach. There was just terrible silence, much like her life was these days.

She nodded and occasionally spoke to familiar faces as she walked along the beach walk but didn't feel ready to engage in frivolous conversation. Friends had always said she never met a stranger, but suddenly everyone was a stranger to her.

The first year following Alex's death she had considered moving, but the tall towers of The Shores had held her heart from the first day they were fortunate enough to visit. The twinkling lights from the condos in the many different buildings made every night seem like Christmas. When the fog came in, as it often did, the buildings were engulfed in a deep mist of shadows and clouds. The many keys to her condo took some getting used to, but the lifestyle gave her a secure feeling at the water's edge, and she never tired of the view. From the guard at the gate to the doorman in the lobby, she felt safe and secure.

Little did she know someone she was once close to had targeted her family for revenge; someone who, unknown to Meredith, had been stalking her for almost a year.

Her daughters called often, but Meredith tried not to lean on them. They were also suffering from the loss of their father and had to get back in the swing of their busy careers.

Jennifer was kind enough to have her mother help in her stores whenever she was in Palm Springs. Although once the owner of the stores, Meredith smiled to herself thinking Jen had become the boss many years before. The business had moved on and all the clubs and organizations she had been a member of were still active but with younger women at the helm—women whose names she didn't even know.

Meredith gradually began spending her days playing bridge and having lunch with her many San Diego and Coronado friends. Her phone rang constantly with kindhearted invitations, and there was a steady stream of out-of-towners who always enjoyed a local city tour.

Slowly her world seemed to be righting itself with more trips, social events, and even an occasional dinner with a gentleman set up by a well-meaning friend. She laughed when she thought of all the different men her friends thought might interest her. So often dinner would begin cordially with a handshake and small talk, then progress to the gentleman's past life which usually consisted of either a deceased wife or his miserable relationship with his ex. When she was asked about her married life she found it hard to explain a lifetime of love to someone who was just trying to make pleasant dinner conversation.

Everyone was trying hard but Meredith. It was easier to stay home and sit on the large patio reading a book or staring at her beautiful ocean. She seldom poured wine for herself these days as drinking alone now made her melancholy and wine gave her a bit of a headache. Her evening cocktail became tonic and lime, minus the gin, and in her heart, she was sharing it with Alex.

Walking became a morning ritual both for exercise and weight control. Meredith wanted to maintain her appearance. "It's my cover," she was quick to tell her daughters. She painted her toes in bright coral polish and went for a manicure twice a month. Hands and feet had always been important to her, and she smiled remembering the hours spent rubbing potions on Alex's large feet and wished those size fourteen shoes were still under her bed.

29

Jennifer took over Meredith's finances. Nothing seemed to change except the signature on the check. She ensured the bills were paid on time and gave her mother a monthly allowance, part of which went to keeping her blonde, always important to a California girl.

To an outsider looking in, it would seem Meredith had a perfect life. But to her, she was perfectly alone. Nights were always the worst when her tired eyes filled with tears as she lay by herself in their bed. She needed to find a way to stop the loneliness.

Desperate for a change of scenery, Meredith decided it was time to venture to the Big Apple Claire had called home for years, and she planned a trip to New York to see her daughter and granddaughter, Heather Ann.

Their youngest daughter, Claire, had been a beautiful child and grew to be a stunning woman. She graduated third in her high school class but found college to be more challenging. Arizona State University in Tempe was known as one of the top party schools in the country, and sorority and fraternity fun took its toll on Claire's grade point average.

Then came the visit from Alex and Meredith. Her father began sternly, "Young lady, your grades are not up to your normal standards."

Followed by her mother, "I understand the excitement of being away from home for the first time, but this simply won't do. You need to buckle down and study."

Her dad was even more explicit. "No excuses. This university costs a great deal. I understand wanting to have fun, but if you don't learn to balance studies and fun, you will be financing your own education."

Claire felt the tears begin to run down her face. "I'm sorry, Mom and Dad. You're both right, I have played too much and know my grades have suffered. College is so different from high school   there's so much freedom, so many activities, all my new friends."

Meredith started to reach for her daughter but Alex shook his head and whispered, "Be strong."

"Claire," he said, "We think this school is too big and has too many distractions. Your mother and I want you to transfer to someplace smaller. We will support you for one more school year. If things don't improve after that, you are on your own."

Unfortunately, her low grades meant she was not able to transfer to one of her preferred east coast schools, but she was accepted to the University of San Diego. Once settled in her new environment and with renewed commitments to her studies, she began to focus on a future career and decided law was the direction she wanted to take.

She knew the path to a law license was long and hard, so she added study times for the law school admissions test to the classwork for her major, political science. By the time she was eligible to take the actual test, she passed on her first attempt. Thanks to her now-excellent grades and some first-hand experience gained during a part-time job with a local law firm, Claire was accepted to Columbia Law School in New York City, her number one choice.

Of course, there were a couple of surprising bumps in the road on the way to her law degree. One was the increase in the level of time and energy her classes required, and the second was fellow law student, David Armstrong.

They married during their final year at Columbia and daughter Heather Ann was born a year later, followed within months by graduation and a job with a small family law firm in the heart of New York City. It had been a long road, but she was finally a practicing attorney.

Her personal life did not go as smoothly as her professional life. Claire's marriage to David collapsed amicably nine years after it began, leaving her as Heather Ann's primary parent. Sadly, three years later David was killed in a car accident and Claire became her daughter's sole support. But her beauty was also an asset and she was soon seen at New York social gatherings on the arms of very influential men.

As the plane landed at JFK, Meredith knew being with Claire and Heather Ann would be a wonderful distraction for her, and their tearful reunion at the airport showed her how much they had all missed each other. With their arms wrapped around one another, Meredith was in heaven with her *far-away girls* as she called Heather Ann and Claire.

After a harrowing cab ride from the airport and a brief lunch, Claire began showing off her adopted city. She introduced Meredith to the colleagues at her law firm and then proudly to her New York home. Claire and her daughter were settled into a beautiful apartment and it made Meredith rest easier knowing they were safe in such a big city. Claire had found a progressive, accelerated school not far from the apartment for Heather Ann, who had already made numerous friends.

The three attended an evening production of *A Chorus Line*, and a matinee of the smash hit *The Lion King*, which Heather Ann dearly adored.

Claire loved sharing favorite restaurants with Meredith and taking her shopping for wardrobe updates. Claire had always been a fashion plate and gave her mother the feeling she was less than chic, although Meredith felt she had quite enough *chic* for her casual beach lifestyle. They browsed through designer shops on Fifth Avenue, all a bit too expensive for Meredith, but she went willingly just to be with her beautiful daughter.

By the end of her five-day visit, Meredith was exhausted from shopping and had eaten too much rich food, but being able to tuck Heather Ann in bed each night made everything worthwhile. It was the best time of the day for Meredith.

When Claire dropped her at JFK for the return trip to San Diego, Meredith was exhausted but much more comfortable with the life her daughter had embraced for herself and Heather Ann.

Made even busier since it was a weekend, Meredith navigated across the concourse toward gate 26 to board her flight home. As she made her way,

Meredith caught a glimpse of a tall well-built man in a dark business suit headed in the opposite direction toward the exit door and the street. She stopped and turned for a moment, but with all the crowds it was difficult to see more of him.

He looked vaguely familiar. Did she know him? Should she know him? Was he a business associate of Alex's? Through the glass doors of the airport, Meredith could see only the side of his face as he entered the waiting town car at the curb. He reminded her of someone she knew long ago and her feelings surged but, in a minute, he was gone.

After settling into her seat bound for home her mind drifted again to the distinguished man she had seen on the concourse. She felt she knew him but couldn't place him. As her eyes slowly closed it came to her. He reminded Meredith of her old college boyfriend, Paul Richardson. But that man couldn't be Paul; the last she had heard, he was still doing construction work in Arizona. The man she had seen getting into the back seat of a town car in New York City was impeccably dressed and had the look of a business executive. As sleep overtook her, after the busy days spent with Claire and Heather Ann, the mysterious man was forgotten and Meredith dozed the rest of the flight.

Soon after returning from New York City, summer visitors began to arrive at The Shores and Meredith was thrilled to see her many out-of-state friends. Life became a bit more social and she was suddenly busy, with little time to think until she went upstairs to her condo where once again she would sit alone.

She knew down deep something had to change. "I'm drowning," she heard herself say out loud. "Oh my God, I have started talking to myself, and it's not the first time." She had to get back to the land of the living. Her family could only be used as crutches for so long.

She considered getting a part-time job. After all, she had been a successful salesperson all her life, smiling as she remembered her days as a clerk in the Walgreens cosmetic department where she first dusted shelves and learned to display merchandise. But she soon realized *experience* was not what merchants were looking for today. They wanted younger clerks.

She could run circles around most salespeople of any age, but truth be told she realized, *age did matter*. Frustrated, she gave up the idea after a few interviews.

Still in need of something to help her pass the time, she followed a friend's suggestion and looked into places that needed volunteers. Meredith found herself most interested in a position at a local library. She loved books and enjoyed learning about the intricacies of a library. She checked out books for readers and re-shelved books for librarians. She even led the children's storytimes occasionally. The hours spent at the library helped her days go smoother and Meredith slowly began to realize, while she still ached for Alex, she was beginning to smile again.

CHAPTER 4

Widow. Meredith had been wearing that word like a badge. To her, the three years since she lost Alex were the longest she had lived during her sixty-plus on earth. For all her family's good intentions, none of them had been able to fill the giant crater in her heart named Alex.

She could no longer fill her days with mindless card games, luncheons, and volunteer time at the library. She had refused many invitations from longtime friends who wanted to see her and knew they would stop calling if she didn't accept their offers occasionally. She felt adrift and knew she needed a change of scenery.

Alex's estate enabled her to pay off the mortgage on the condominium and her tax accountant told her if she watched her spending, she would be financially sound for many years to come. She had travel funds and it was time to use them.

The first person Meredith thought to call was her lifelong friend Karen Hall, now Doctor Karen Hall and one of the Directors at the Bureau of Medical Services at the US State Department in Washington, DC. As busy and important as she was, Karen adjusted her calendar for her dear friend's arrival in the middle of September. Meredith planned to play tourist and see all of the DC sights as she had with Alex years before.

Assessing her closet Meredith realized her wardrobe consisted of casual beachwear not geared to life in Washington, DC, the political capital of the world. Following her New York experience, she knew it was time to go shopping, as she wanted to fit in and not embarrass her important friend.

She enjoyed going through the boutiques on Orange Avenue and putting together a few additions to the items she had purchased with Claire in New York. She even spent a day browsing the shops of the Fashion Valley Mall. Recalling the unwritten rule that women's fashion in DC be either navy blue or black, she bought a couple of items, darker than her usual bright beach attire, then lunched at the Nordstrom's Café enjoying her favorite tomato bisque soup, and apple-pear salad.

The two friends had traveled together many times, and she smiled thinking about their trip to Cape Cod. The trip had turned into a hilarious disaster. She had left Karen in charge of reservations since the arrangements had to be made through her office in DC. Karen wanted to stay in a bed and breakfast, and the government had agreed.

The room they were assigned was on the second floor of a beautifully converted historic home with no elevator and one queen-size bed. Never known for traveling light, Meredith looked between the stairs, her luggage, and Karen, and asked, "So, where is the bellman?" Karen just shook her head, picked up her single suitcase, and headed up the stairs.

The first night was spent rolling into each other in the too-small bed. More than once, the words *roll over* were heard in the dark.

The second night Meredith decided to fix the situation. "I'm going to make a bed divider out of towels so we can get some sleep."

Skeptically, Karen said, "Don't you think the bed is already small enough? If you put a row of towels down the center we will both be hugging the edges all night."

Undaunted, Meredith took the big, fluffy towels from the bathroom, rolled them up into long tubes, and placed them on the bed. "Now, tonight we can each stay on our side."

She didn't glance up in time to see Karen roll her eyes.

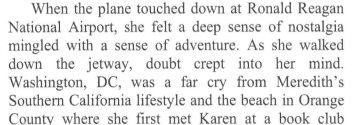

When the plane touched down at Ronald Reagan National Airport, she felt a deep sense of nostalgia mingled with a sense of adventure. As she walked down the jetway, doubt crept into her mind. Washington, DC, was a far cry from Meredith's Southern California lifestyle and the beach in Orange County where she first met Karen at a book club hosted by a mutual friend. Had this been the right thing to do?

Then she saw Karen waiting to meet her in the baggage claim area and her doubts vanished. They hugged, shed more than a few tears, and walked arm in arm to the waiting black town car Meredith thought might belong to the government. She sensed her friend must be more important than she realized.

Karen lived in a quiet neighborhood in Alexandria, Virginia, about forty minutes from her State Department office. Tall green elm trees lined the streets, and each home sat proudly, knowing it had weathered the test of time. The lush greenery surrounding her home gave a warm yet elegant feeling to the established area.

She helped Meredith settle into her comfortable guestroom decorated in provincial colors of blue and white and lots of lace. Meredith unpacked, hung her clothes, and together they laughed at how old they were and how many years they had been friends.

They knew everything about one another. Well, that wasn't quite true. Karen knew all of Meredith's secrets, but with each new promotion in the State Department, Karen's life had become more and more highly classified.

Meredith smiled as she recalled Karen's photo taken the night she met Her Majesty, Queen Elizabeth II of England. They laughed about the *famous* blue sequined dress Karen had been so proud to wear. She had never looked more beautiful; her head held high and back so straight, she looked regal herself.

While Karen led an exciting professional life, her personal life had not been as successful. Although she dated off and on, Karen needed to maintain so many secrets there wasn't much time or space for personal relationships, or so it seemed.

Karen and Meredith both agreed she needed a

man but Karen laughed, telling Meredith that traveling in her current social circles with all those people keeping track of their own restricted lives, she would never meet a man.

"If I found one," Karen said, "he would be married, and that is strictly off-limits in my position."

"It's a shame the Vice President isn't single," Meredith joked. "He is so handsome."

Karen smiled to herself wondering just how her old friend had come so near to one of her most guarded secrets. The trips on Air Force Two were some of the biggest adventures of her life.

Her affair with Vice President Carl Stapleton had begun over eight years ago when he was a United States Senator. Of course, he was married, not happily he said, but he needed a strong image. His wife was of good Boston stock, and her pedigree was important to ensure his credibility, according to what he told Karen.

It didn't take long for Karen and Carl to fall in love and there always seemed to be a need for her to travel with him. If there wasn't a specific reason, he would create one. She was in too deep and too much in love to alter their situation. Their affair became the most important secret Karen had to keep.

Over the years the two friends had joked about Meredith entrusting Alex to Karen on the sheer chance she died first. Now here they sat, drinking tea and each thinking of him and wishing he was there sitting between them. Sensing Meredith's sorrow, Karen, tried to bring a smile to her dear friend's face. But when she reached her arm around Meredith's shoulder, the tears flowed and they cried for the wonderful man they had both loved and lost.

Karen Hall was a true Southern beauty—Southern Texas, that is. She was a world-class violinist. But instead of sharing her musical genius with the world, she shared it with private students as she continued her studies in psychiatry.

Becoming a Doctor of Psychiatry cost her a marriage and she divorced in 1985. She had two sons. Kevin had followed in her footsteps and was now a prominent therapist on the east coast, but she had lost contact with her younger son Randy many years before. She was unable to stay close to them or anyone else due to her high government security clearances. International assignments didn't make for warm and fuzzy home visits.

Karen had encouraged Meredith and Alex to visit her while she was attached to the American Embassy in Nairobi, but they declined. The jungles of Africa held no interest for Meredith who was terrified of even the smallest bug or animal. They did however spend two glorious weeks with her in London the following year.

She had lived all over the world and had been in danger many times. Karen was lucky to be traveling to the Evans home for Alex's birthday party on September 7, 1998, when the American Embassy in Nairobi was destroyed, and 224 people were killed. She lost twelve of her State Department co-workers and many friends at the Embassy in the bombing the al Qaeda terrorist organization claimed responsibility for. After the attack, Karen was re-assigned to Washington, DC, as there was nothing left of her office, not even her desk.

Meredith always wondered how she, Karen, and Alex, had stayed close for so many years. It takes work to maintain friendships, she used to tell Alex, and the past three years had certainly taught her the value of her many true friends.

Meredith had always thought her next visit to the Nation's Capital would be during cherry blossom season, but this was September, and signs of fall were beginning to appear. The city still looked impressive and other than much longer lines at the monuments, she enjoyed touring the nation's capital. However, after two full days on the Mall and in the various Smithsonian museums, she realized her patience had grown too thin to put up with all the crowds.

Karen had accepted a couple of social invitations for the two of them, one a small cocktail party, and the second a dinner party at the home of a fellow State Department crony. Anticipating a special event, Meredith had come prepared with her favorite beige dinner suit. The suit would suffice for any occasion and she planned to drink only white wine or gin, ensuring spills would not leave a spot.

Wednesday, the first cocktail party was to begin at 6:30 p.m. A bit tired from standing in long lines at The Smithsonian, Meredith quickly showered and was ready when Karen arrived home.

Karen called out to her, "Are you ready to leave?"

"Dressed and ready to meet the troops," Meredith replied with a salute and a laugh.

Meredith felt quite luxurious seated beside her important friend in a car driven by a government driver. But she decided after her first fifteen minutes at the party that government employees speak a private language, one an outsider would never understand.

The party-goers were polite to the houseguest of their superior but remained reserved. Meredith thought of her son, Stephen, his secret government life, and never being able to discuss day-to-day business activities with his wife, Loren—a harsh contrast to the intimate details she had shared daily with Alex. As Meredith extended her hand to one of Karen's department heads she thought about how complicated government life was.

She was careful when selecting her first glass of white wine from the tray being passed by a smiling waiter. She didn't want to spill on her only cocktail suit. The hors d'oeuvres were light but filling and were to be dinner she guessed as she ate her third canapé.

Karen and Meredith left the party early, claiming important morning meetings for Karen, but both knew the meeting was at Tyson's Corner in Fairfax, Virginia, just outside of DC. They had a frivolous day of shopping planned.

Meredith couldn't wait to quiz her friend about some of the interesting people she had met. Her first comment made Karen roar with laughter. "They talk in circles and never say anything," Meredith said with a smile in her voice.

"We can't," Karen answered. "Our lives are so secret sometimes we don't understand them ourselves." Meredith laughed with her friend, and they settled back for the short ride home.

Arriving back at Karen's, they realized they were both still hungry. When Meredith saw Karen's refrigerator was no better stocked than hers she laughed. "My children call me the queen of condiments. I can dress up the best takeout food and add to a sandwich providing it needs nothing more than mustard or mayo." Looking in the refrigerator she couldn't even find something to put between two slices of bread. They ended the evening dining on Meredith's favorite snack—hot chocolate and cinnamon toast, a trick Jennifer once shared when she came in late from the stores.

While sitting at the small kitchen table they laughed like teenagers and spoke of clothes, styles, exercising, the latest movies Meredith knew Karen would never make time to see, and inevitably, men.

Karen asked Meredith, "How's your love life?"

"Non-existent," Meredith replied.

"Sounds just like mine!" Karen laughed. "I think maybe that's something we both need to correct."

"It's not quite as simple to meet men as it used to be. I have been on a few dates set up by well-meaning friends, but I was never quite comfortable with any of those men, and I certainly have no desire to try Internet dating. I wouldn't even know where to begin."

"I agree," Karen said. "Well, we aren't going to

45

solve this problem tonight. Let's call it an evening and get some rest so we are ready to shop tomorrow."

Meredith glanced at the clock and felt guilty keeping Karen up so late, but knew both of them had enjoyed the evening and their cinnamon toast. Once in a while, it was good for Karen to laugh. Meredith thought it probably didn't happen often for the serious woman with the demanding job and secretive lifestyle.

They decided to sleep late, late for Karen at least, and spend the afternoon at Tyson's Corners, one of Karen's favorite shopping spots. The mall was calling her name and by eleven o'clock they were off for a day of fun. As they walked out the door Meredith turned to Karen and said, "Let's see if we can each find something dazzling for the party tomorrow night that will knock the starch out of those stiff government types."

With a smile, Karen replied, "We are rather boring at times, aren't we?"

The shopping center, an area favorite, was anchored by Neiman Marcus and Nordstrom. Over the years, stores had come and gone and had been updated frequently to both remain in step with the times and enhance the shopping experience. Through all the years and changes, beautiful boutiques continued welcoming customers with elaborate window displays and excellent sales staff. It was easy to recognize that the stores and their staff were used to catering to the rich, famous, and very important.

They spent the afternoon roaming through the mall, stopping occasionally for coffees and light snacks, and in several stores looking for the perfect dresses to dazzle boring government types. They tried on a few outfits, always asking the salesperson to put them next to each other in the dressing rooms. When Karen came out to show off one of her choices Meredith almost doubled over in laughter. "That's one of the ugliest dresses I have ever seen. I can't imagine having *any* fun wearing it."

Looking at herself in the three-panel mirror, Karen also began laughing and said, "Oh, you're right. It looked so much better on the hanger."

In the end, Karen bought an expensive suit and Meredith found a perfect non-DC outfit at Nordstrom's. Both girls justified their purchases with the age-old adage *they were on sale*. After a trip around the Neiman Marcus cosmetic counter, the two tired friends passed up dinner in a restaurant for a quick pick-up salad at Karen's favorite deli.

Back at the house they modeled their bargains and laughed at the bulges they were trying to hide. As she turned to the left and right showing off her new purchase, Meredith said with a laugh, "Well, my outfit won't do for a fancy State Department party. I'll have to wear the same suit I wore to the cocktail party."

"Oh, you'll look beautiful regardless of what you wear," Karen told her. "I think you'll enjoy yourself tomorrow evening. And you never know who you may meet," Karen teased. "We did a lot of walking today and I have to be at work early in the morning. I am going to say good night." With a brief hug and a kiss, Karen turned toward her bedroom.

Taking a cue from her friend, Meredith also

headed to her room. Both women were asleep by nine, completely exhausted.

Karen left for her office at six the next morning and Meredith spent the day reading and even snuck in a short nap. She was enjoying all the fun but felt guilty for taking so much of her busy friend's time. But she would be leaving in the late afternoon the following day and was having a wonderful visit. She was so glad to have ventured out into the world beyond the small island she called home.

Meredith worried about wearing her simple beige suit to the State Department dinner but knew it would have to do. As she fastened the last button on her jacket, she prayed the same guests were not attending tonight's dinner as had been at the previous cocktail party. Then Meredith laughed to herself because, as boring as those guests were, they would likely not remember her, much less what she had worn the previous night.

Just as she finished dressing, the telephone rang. Karen was held up with a crisis at the office and was sending the car for Meredith. She would meet her at the party and promised to be there as soon as possible. Meredith was hesitant, but Karen reassured her she would do fine on her own.

"Just talk about the President," she said. "It always gets the conversation going."

Within fifteen minutes the car arrived, and Meredith soon found herself standing on the steps of yet another beautiful Georgetown home. Lush grounds and seasonal flowers were everywhere in the manicured gardens.

She took a deep breath and rang the bell. She was greeted by a distinguished butler wearing a fitted black waistcoat and white gloves. Did everyone in DC have a butler, she wondered? Following a quick check of the guest list, "Mrs. Meredith Evans, guest of Director Karen Hall," was announced and she was ushered into a large reception area.

She stood staring at the beautiful room. Fine antiques were everywhere, and large elegant tapestries covered the walls. She recognized many of the custom-selected fabrics of silk, rich satin, and twisted brocade that covered the chairs and settees.

Meredith felt shy amongst the elaborate surroundings and wished Karen was there to introduce her to her fellow dinner companions. She asked for the hostess and was introduced to a woman in her early sixties, well-rounded everywhere. Upon extending her hand Meredith received a warm welcome and an interest in herself she had not expected.

Celeste Sutherland had been married to Walter Sutherland, a Washington Bureau Chief for the State Department for thirty-five years, and had met Karen when they were both assigned to the American Embassy in London. The Sutherlands had been transferred to the DC area two years ago and Walter had just finished important international negotiations in Saudi Arabia. They had lived all over the world and Meredith enjoyed listening to Celeste's comments on their various residences and family of five children.

She asked and seemed quite interested in Meredith's retail background and admitted shopping was her favorite pastime. As Meredith's eyes scanned the room, she could imagine her hostess doing just that.

As she and Celeste were finishing their conversation, a butler interrupted with a message from Karen. She had been delayed again and would not arrive until dinner at seven-thirty.

Accepting a glass of white wine served in a Baccarat crystal-stemmed glass from a roaming waiter, Meredith walked through the room toward the terrace. She surveyed the elegant women in expensive designer clothes, their arms linked to men as if to say, "He's mine."

After a few minutes of meaningless conversation with various groups, she continued toward the terrace and as she was about to step through the French doors stopped in her tracks. Walking toward her was a familiar face, the face she had seen in the New York airport a few months before.

The man making his way in from the terrace also stopped as if he had recognized her.

Meredith was afraid to speak. What if she was wrong and it wasn't him? She stood rooted to the spot wondering if the man could be Paul Richardson.

As he smiled and continued walking towards her, Meredith reached for a chair to steady herself, trying to gather her composure.

He was older, grayer, and taller than she remembered, and incredibly handsome.

He stopped a few feet from her and extended his hand. He couldn't believe his eyes as he gazed at the elegant woman standing before him. Could this be the girl he had declared his love to on that deserted riverbank so many years ago?

"Hello, I'm Paul Richardson," he said. "I know this is an old line, but have we met somewhere before?"

He saw a smile of recognition cross her face and the scene of their last encounter flooded into his memory. She had been the driving force in his life without even knowing it. His mind was racing, and he was trying to gather his wits to not make a fool of himself.

"I think we have more than met, Paul. I'm Meredith Jamison Evans," she said extending her hand.

They stood close, each afraid to say a word, and at the same moment realized they were still clutching each other's hands. Meredith found herself speechless, a rare thing for her. What had brought them together and why here in DC?

"I don't believe this, Meredith. It's been more than forty years."

Before Meredith could respond, Karen came rushing towards them spilling over with apologies for being late. Karen realized in an instant she had interrupted something but was not sure just what. Meredith released Paul's hand and introduced him.

"Karen, this is Paul Richardson, an old friend I have not seen in many years."

To Meredith's surprise, Karen smiled and reached for Paul's extended hand, "Great to see you again, Paul, but after the day I've had, I really need a drink." The tension in the Far East was at warp speed and seven of her staffers, situated in the wrong place, were in serious danger. She quickly excused herself and headed towards the bar.

As she turned to greet one of her department heads, she glanced back in the direction of her dear friend. Wouldn't that be some duo, she thought, but was quick to bring the conversation back to the troubles in the Far East.

On the far side of the room near the terrace, Meredith and Paul stood trying to come to grips with their sudden unexpected meeting. Meredith clutched her glass of white wine and prayed Paul couldn't see her hand was shaking. Where had he been all these years and how did this politically correct city find it in its heart to bring them together?

Meredith found she was staring into the eyes of the football hero who had wanted her love so many years ago. Was he remembering their last meeting as she was?

Her mind raced, but she gathered her courage, took a deep breath, and spoke at the exact moment Paul began. They both laughed at their uncomfortable behavior. Paul insisted she go first, and she had just begun telling him why she was in DC when a waiter announced dinner was served. They stood for an extra moment as if to memorize the new face of the aging other. Neither wanted to break the spell of their reunion, but this was Washington, DC, and everything ran on a schedule.

As Meredith turned, searching for Karen, Paul offered her his arm and smiled, "May I escort you to dinner?" adding he hoped they might be seated at the same table. When they reached the dining room, they found their place cards were at opposite ends of the room, but he assured her they would catch up later.

Her eyes followed Paul to his table where he was seated between two beautiful women, one his wife she assumed, as he quickly engaged in conversation with her.

Karen and Meredith were seated with Municipal Court Judge Harry Slater and his wife, Virginia; Ohio Congressman Michael O'Malley and his wife Constance; and US Senator Gerald Ferguson from the great state of Texas. Meredith wanted to pinch herself to prove she was here and in the presence of such exciting company and within a few moments, they all joined in typical Washington conversation.

She couldn't help but notice the impeccable way the table was set. After all, tabletop had been her business for almost thirty years. Each name had been scripted on a porcelain place card and the china place settings were exquisite. A large ruby red charger trimmed in gold held an ivory dinner plate with the Sutherland crest adorning the center.

She had not seen this much sterling silver since her tour of Buckingham Palace. Thank goodness years of selling fine china had taught her which fork to use, as there were many to choose from. Meredith eyed the Buccellati flatware and recognized her favorite Val St. Lambert crystal stemware.

She smiled remembering all the tables she had set. She had even competed in charity fundraising events in her small desert town and her store windows won prizes year after year. But it was nothing in comparison to her surroundings tonight. As she assessed the cost of each place setting she decided government service paid quite well.

As Meredith reached for her napkin Karen leaned

towards her asking, "Just how do you know Paul?"

"You seemed quite friendly yourself," Meredith replied. "You almost gave him a kiss on the cheek."

Karen smiled her famous broad Texas smile and replied, "Well, he is one of the largest building contractors in the country and is as nice a man as he is gorgeous."

Yes, she was right about the gorgeous part, Meredith thought, as she listened to her friend's continued conversation.

"He does a lot of government work. He worked on the rebuild of the wing of the Pentagon damaged during the September 11 attack, and just finished a project for the State Department."

Before she could continue, they were interrupted by a waiter serving a wedge salad topped with pungent blue cheese that looked almost too pretty to eat. The main course, rack of lamb, was done to perfection and she was so happy when all the other diners at her table picked up the small ribs and devoured every last bit from the bones.

Daring a glance toward Paul's table, she saw him deep in conversation with the redhead on his right. He was laughing now, she noticed, thinking how he looked so important seated between the two elegant ladies.

Just how does one go from football hero to construction king? No wonder those women are drooling over him. Meredith leaned towards Karen and whispered they would continue their assessment of Paul on the way home, and with that, they settled into a chatty dinner conversation. Karen was right. Just bring up the President, and everyone thinks you are one of them.

More than once during dinner Meredith glanced across the room straight into Paul's eyes. As she stared at him, she remembered her recent visit with Claire and the distinguished man she had seen at the airport. The more she studied him, the more convinced she became that it had indeed been Paul she had seen in New York.

She found it hard to concentrate on the conversation at her table, interesting as it was. She couldn't believe the surprising events of the evening. Paul seemed to know most of the dignitaries in the room, was comfortable among them, and was no doubt well connected in Washington circles.

As she glanced his way again, his eyes held hers. He was almost flirting with her and she couldn't take her eyes off him. He reminded her of a Western cowboy. Tough, strong, macho, and yes, drop-dead gorgeous, to quote Karen. She tore her eyes away and forced herself to listen to the boring conversation of legislation passed by Congress the past week.

She should have been interested in the discussion, but her mind was spinning down a dusty road to meet a former boyfriend. Their lives had gone in such different directions since the day she had refused their affair. He had wanted her, and she had wanted him, but they both did the right thing. They walked away and stayed away, until tonight.

Across the room, trying to concentrate on his Cherries Jubilee, Paul's mind was also racing. He too was thinking back to the secluded river's edge with its weeping willow trees that wrapped the two lovers in a dark and secret net.

He studied the face of the woman he had loved and lost but sworn never to forget. Just where had life taken her the last forty years? Had she stayed with her husband, had other children? Most of all, he wondered just what had brought her to DC?

One by one the guests rose to enjoy an after-dinner brandy on the terrace. Paul refused the coffee being served. Meredith, on the other hand, treated herself to a cup of decaf coffee poured by a waiter carrying an ornate coffee pot she recognized as her favorite sterling silver pattern, Grande Baroque. When she finished her coffee, she excused herself and left Karen deep in conversation with Senator Ferguson over something she felt was too important for her to hear about.

She walked towards the terrace to enjoy the view of the beautiful city and all its lights. Meredith hoped Karen knew how lucky she was to live in this magical place.

"A beautiful night," someone said from behind, and she didn't have to turn to know it was Paul. "Would you care for an after-dinner drink?" he asked in a low voice.

Meredith quietly declined, "No, thank you." She might need a clear head to look into those dark eyes she was beginning to remember. He had been a kind and simple young man when the biggest thing on his mind was winning the next football game or how to get her into the back seat of his '57 Chevy.

Paul took a deep breath and asked her how long she planned to be in DC. Meredith turned to him. "I'm leaving tomorrow afternoon."

"I would love to spend the rest of the evening catching up on our last forty years, but I have a six a.m. meeting with some heavy hitters on Pennsylvania Avenue. Would you have time for lunch before your flight leaves?" he added.

"What would your wife say?" she responded.

"Well, if I had one, I would hope she would understand lunch with an old friend, but since I don't, it's you I have to worry about. What would your husband think?"

Meredith's eyes dropped to her left hand. "I am a widow, Paul." It's just lunch with an old friend, she thought, a friend who had once loved her. Her reply came so fast she surprised herself. "I am staying with Karen and I live in San Diego on Coronado Island. My flight leaves at five p.m. from Reagan National and I think lunch would be perfect."

Paul reached into his pocket and handed her his business card. "If you have any second thoughts call any of these numbers. Mrs. Parker, my executive assistant, will know how and where to reach me. I do hope you'll come."

Just then Karen walked up, two purses in hand, to tell Meredith the car was waiting. "Paul and I are having lunch together before I leave tomorrow," Meredith announced.

Karen smiled at her friend. "Would you like me to arrange for the private dining room at the Hyatt near the airport? It would be a wonderful way to end your trip to DC."

Paul took Karen's extended hand and said, "Great to have friends in high places. Many thanks and I hope you will urge Meredith to keep our date."

Meredith looked at him surprised as if to question whether their lunch was indeed a *date*.

The three of them paid their respects to the hostess and proceeded to the steps of the Sutherland home where Karen's government vehicle waited. Paul reached for the door and Karen entered the car first. Meredith turned to say good night to Paul. Neither touched.

"Please meet me tomorrow," he said as she leaned into the car. Meredith smiled, entered the car, and waved as the car pulled onto M Street.

Paul stood there staring after the car carrying the woman he had once loved as it drove away. This time it wasn't the deserted riverbank, and they were on equal ground. No, that was not quite true. She was on his turf now. He was successful and her equal.

He would find a way to have her back in his life. Nothing would stop him this time.

The two women were no more than around the corner when Karen started quizzing Meredith as to, "just what was going on between you and that handsome Paul Richardson."

Meredith gave her a brief synopsis of her surprising evening. She was quick to add Paul was not married now due to circumstances not yet known. She promised to call Karen with all the juicy details after lunch the following day. They both laughed at the idea of even having juicy details to share.

Arriving home, they hugged each other and agreed to continue their conversation in the morning.

Meredith undressed, looking into the mirror at the simple beige suit she had worn to tonight's event. She had never considered herself a beauty but was always well put together, as her friends would say. As she folded the suit carefully back into the suitcase, she was pleased it had made it through two social events. She closed the case and slipped into bed, content she was ready for tomorrow.

But was she?

She tossed and turned thinking of the uncertain day ahead. She finally pulled the warm covers up and recited her favorite line from Miss Scarlett O'Hara, *tomorrow is another day*. Then she rolled over, tucked the blankets tightly under her chin, and was soon asleep.

CHAPTER 5

Meredith heard Karen's alarm go off early the next morning. She knew from her few comments at dinner last night her office was in crisis. Having company added stress for someone in Karen's position, and Meredith felt she had taken her friend away from the office far too long. Karen came out to the kitchen ready to leave for her office with little time to linger.

Over a quick cup of coffee, the two old friends promised to talk soon about Meredith's impending date with Paul, but Meredith felt her luncheon would be forgotten as Karen resumed her busy schedule. They hugged and cried, as was their usual goodbye, and then Dr. Karen Hall rushed to her waiting car and what seemed her only love, the State Department of the United States Government.

Meredith dressed in her favorite travel attire, black velvet sweats with just the right touch of gold stitching around her slender neck. Underneath she sported a gold cashmere turtleneck. Meredith had a four and half hour flight back to San Diego and the weather would be cool when she arrived. She would be the most overdressed person on the plane but was proud she still turned heads with her classy appearance and knew she always looked first class even when traveling coach.

Knowing she would be dining at the Hyatt's private dining room concerned her but she dressed the sweats up with jewelry—three single gold bangle bracelets around her wrist and the diamond solitaire necklace Alex had given her on their thirtieth wedding anniversary. With her suitcases in tow, she looked every bit the part of a sophisticated traveler.

She was nervous as she rolled her suitcases to the door and glanced one last time in the hall mirror. She had not called Paul to cancel their lunch, so presumed he would be expecting her. Lunch in a beautiful hotel awaited her and if she had to eat alone, so be it. Through the front window of Karen's house, she saw her taxi pull to the curb. She was on her way.

The valet at the Hyatt Crystal City opened the cab door and helped her out. He walked her towards the lobby check-in counter to drop off her bags to be held while she enjoyed lunch and she then asked him to direct her to the hotel's exclusive dining room.

Her soft black walking shoes glided across the marble floor of the hotel lobby. She felt she didn't belong in these sterile, but opulent surroundings. This was Karen's world. She thought how good it would be to return to her comfortable and casual life at the beach. She was ready to go home, but first, a girl did have to eat.

A private elevator took her to the tenth floor. She stepped out into the restaurant lobby and saw Paul waiting at the entrance. He was impeccably dressed in a dark black business suit, white shirt, and steel gray tie that accented his dark hair touched with gray at the temples. He smiled as she approached, held out his hand, and greeted her.

He was quite a handsome package, she thought, and could not control the smile that crossed her face, nor did she want to.

"I am so glad you came," he said, as they were ushered to their table in a secluded corner of the room. Paul reached to take her arm at the elbow in much the same manner Alex had always done. It felt comfortable, almost as if Alex were walking beside her.

The maître d' held her chair and after sitting down she glanced out the window at the beautiful view of DC, thinking how strange it was so many of the buildings seemed close to the same height.

Paul noticed her look of confusion. When Meredith told him what had caught her eyes, he smiled and said, "DC has a height restriction for buildings."

She returned his smile and then became aware of how few tables were in the area where the two of them had been seated. More of Karen's handiwork, she guessed and wasn't surprised.

Fresh flowers adorned the table, which was set with sterling silver flatware and sparkling white china. The settings were a complement to the deep tan walls and thick forest green carpet. She was sure she recognized a couple of United State Senators and even a Congressman who had recently been on television seated nearby. Meredith heard herself say, "This room must be for very important visitors. How do we rate? Do you lunch here often?"

When he smiled to respond, his entire face lit up. "I think it's your famous doctor friend we can thank.

If I had known she had this much pull, I would have asked her out months ago but honestly, shrinks aren't my type." He was quick to add, "Guess that's why I never made it to the company dining room."

The waiter approached to offer them cocktails. Meredith would have loved a gin and tonic to help steady her nerves but ordered a glass of Chardonnay instead. She needed to keep a clear head for this lunch. Paul followed her, ordering a gin and tonic. Meredith's look of surprise caught him off guard. She almost laughed out loud.

"What's so funny?" Paul asked.

"Nothing, it's just gin and tonic has always been our family's drink of choice."

Paul relaxed, sat back in his chair, and smiled. "See, we do have something in common after all these years." Paul reached his long arm across the table and took her hand. "Brought together again by a surprise encounter at a DC dinner party and gin and tonic."

They both laughed, and when their drinks arrived toasted to their chance meeting and the renewal of their friendship.

They ordered lunch, she a Cobb salad and he a fillet of roast beef sandwich. Men and their beef, she thought.

Meredith glanced at her watch aware of her approaching flight and decided it was time to find out more about the handsome man sitting across the table from her. Never known for being shy, she jumped right in. "Where have you been for the last forty years, Paul?"

Paul sat back, smiled, and replied, "Guess that's a

fair question." And so began a most interesting and revealing lunch. To her surprise, he began with the day they last parted.

"After our chance meeting at your apartment complex, and seeing you with your two children, I thought you were the most beautiful woman alive."

Meredith felt herself blush and clutched her hands together under the table.

"I think we are both aware of what happened a month later in our special meeting place at the river's edge. I wasn't sure you would come and when I saw your car drive down what we always called our *private road* my heart stopped.

"I hoped I could hold you in my arms. I needed to kiss you and when we finally melted into one another's arms, the spark between us was too great to be extinguished.

"The way you reacted I knew you wanted me as much as I wanted you. But you stopped. You pushed me away."

"Paul, we were both married."

"Yes, and it took a long time for me to realize you were right. I watched you drive away and out of my life forever, at least I thought so until last night. I was ashamed to go home and face my wife after the lust I had felt through my entire body for you.

"I had loved you since the first time I set eyes on you at the football stadium. I wanted you more that afternoon than I ever thought possible. Desire is a feeling hard to control. But you left me standing alone. So, trying to be the hero I had always thought myself to be, I gathered my macho persona, hopped aboard my trusty Ford pickup, and headed home.

"I drove in a sea of emotions that day. I wanted to cry, and maybe I did with the longing I felt for you. You were right though, our affair would have hurt too many people. We were both married with too many responsibilities.

"I remember pulling into my driveway at home. My two small boys, David and Paul Junior were playing in the front yard. They ran to greet me, and I scooped them both up in my arms. I vowed to become the best father to them I could and continue my life without you. I would channel my feelings for you to them and my wife Rachel.

"Although you and I never made love, I loved you, but that evening as I walked in my front door, you became part of my past."

Meredith was at a loss for words. She was almost afraid to hear more of the secrets he had kept hidden for so many years.

After a long sip of his cocktail, Paul began to speak again.

"As hard as I tried initially, I think Rachel suspected there was someone else. God knows I wanted to be a devoted husband and make her happy. She was a good mother to David and Paul Junior. She spent her time at little league and high school baseball games, tennis matches, and was the Boy Scout father I never was. I could have made time but didn't and we drifted apart."

As the waiter approached their table carrying a full tray, Paul suggested they enjoy their lunch before he continued. He seemed to be deep in his thoughts and as their lunches were placed in front of them, she quickly agreed.

Paul took a bite of his steak sandwich mentioning it would probably be all he would have time for the rest of the day as he was off to more government meetings as soon as their lunch was finished.

Feeling the need to lighten the mood Paul asked what she had done during her visit in DC. Meredith began recounting the museums she had visited, the side trips she and Karen had taken, and the fun evenings they had shared catching up on each other's lives.

Once the table was cleared and coffee had been served, Paul picked up his story where he had left off before lunch was served.

"I took small construction jobs, all I could get my hands on. Two trucks turned into four, then twelve, then twenty. I worked out of our house from the early '70s to 1975, but the business ran out of room and needed more space. I can still remember my first thousand square foot office and the chances I took to make something of myself.

"The seventies had brought new development to the Valley's west side. Dead-end dirt roads and the dusty desert landscape were destined to be part of the new expanding city of Phoenix. I realized roads and infrastructure were needed and purchased my first piece of heavy equipment. Unfortunately, the roads I built drove Rachel and me further apart.

"Within a few years, I had made quite a name for myself in the construction industry. I soon had three Phoenix offices but no time for Rachel or the boys. In an attempt to bring us closer, I suggested we build a new house. The boys and Rachel were so excited, although Rachel and I knew it was primarily for the kids. The house was large by '80s standards with a pool and room for all the boy toys we now owned.

"Rachel had her way with the house. The fun seemed to be in the planning and she had the money to do what she wanted. But soon we were back to our old routine, and of course, the routine wasn't together."

Paul paused in mid-sentence. "Guess I am monopolizing the conversation, but I want to be honest with you about my past."

Meredith looked at him with a half-smile and nodded in thanks.

"I soon had a larger office, more trucks, and I won't lie to you a new woman every few months. Talk about guilt—I was the king of guilt. I know Rachel guessed what was going on, but I felt safe behind the locked doors of my office, and her business remained the boys.

"My first office on the west side was larger than I needed, full of stuff I didn't use, except my secretary. She was cheap like the furniture. No strings, with Rachel being the only person hurt." He watched for a reaction from Meredith but saw none and couldn't figure out just how she was taking his confessions. So, he continued.

"Our name was out there, Richardson Construction Company. More contracts came our way, bigger and more profitable jobs. I expanded in 1979 to Las Vegas and New Mexico. I'm sure you know Vegas meant casinos and hotels, but New Mexico meant the government. Both areas were fountains of business opportunities just waiting to be tapped.

"We started major construction on the new hotels popping up on the Las Vegas strip in the early eighties. We worked on all the Wynn and MGM properties. We had a big stake in Caesars and the Forum Shops and with all our successes, I could have had years of work in Sin City.

"I tried to get Rachel to buy a place in Las Vegas just to have her closer to me, but she preferred to stay in Phoenix. She used the boys as an excuse, but the real truth was she didn't want to be near me.

"During those years she began drinking, something she would later blame on me."

Meredith heard herself say a simple, "I'm sorry."

"Don't be. It was my fault, all of it. I was never there. I know now she was alone by choice but that doesn't make my guilt any less painful." Surprised by his ease in confiding with Meredith, he continued the story, almost relieved to unburden himself and have someone he could trust listen to his private thoughts. The words poured out and he couldn't seem to stop them.

"I landed my first big government contract in 1984, building their secret places in New Mexico, and haven't stopped since. I eventually pulled out of Vegas since government agencies tend to consume you and don't like their big vendors doing business in Sin City.

"Rachel had very few friends, and with both boys out of the house, she drank heavily. I swear I was too busy to notice until it was too late. We seldom fought, as I was never there."

No criticism came from her lips.

"One evening she drank too much, slipped into the pool, and never surfaced."

Meredith's hand rose to her lips. She reached across the table for Paul's hand. She wanted to tell him of her grief and the loss of her brother, but this was not the time. Everyone has their secrets, she thought and remained quiet.

"I can't tell you the guilt I carried for many years, but my sons were my lifesavers. Rachel left a beautiful letter to the boys confessing years of loneliness and unhappiness and stating she had no will to go on. She didn't even mention my name. I think it was her final punishment for the way I had treated her all those years, and she was right." As Paul paused for a sip of his drink, he glanced down at the table.

Meredith felt he was deep in thoughts with the regrets of his past. She didn't know what to say but seemed connected to him without even knowing why. And then he seemed to shake off his mood and again picked up where he had left off.

"Once we got involved with the government in the mid-eighties, we started going international. The construction company is larger than I ever dreamed, demanding all my time. It became my drug of choice. I can't deny we have been successful, but at what price?

"My 1992 contract with the government here in DC sparked an office just off Pennsylvania Avenue. One of our first major government contracts was with the State Department, which is how I came to meet your friend, Dr. Hall.

"Then, after 9/11, their headquarters needed major upgrading for a new security system they were installing and the job required expertise we had in-house. As soon as that project ended, another one came along, then another, and here we are.

"Our RCC trucks are everywhere here in town. My sons, David and PJ, handle most of the contracts with private clients both in the States and around the world, while I focus on the various government agencies that come to us with projects. We were celebrating the closure of another State Department project at the Sutherland home last night."

"Didn't look like a celebration to me," laughed Meredith. "All that restrained behavior in one room and they never smile. But they whisper a lot. Way too serious for me."

"Me too," replied Paul, with a smile so warm Meredith couldn't help but feel nineteen again.

She was quick to add, "You must be very important and very famous, Mr. Richardson."

"I can't deny I have been exceptionally fortunate. Well, that's a quick overview of my last forty years," he added, and what a view it was.

Meredith felt a sudden urge to comfort him. All that success, and yet he seemed so alone. She felt shy in the presence of this very important giant in his industry. Here she sat with an old friend, but not really. An old love, but not a lover. For a brief moment, she wondered what kind of a lover he would have been. She closed her eyes to banish the thought.

As she smiled at him, he couldn't stop himself and reached for her hand, the one not clutching the glass of white wine.

"Tell me about you, Meredith."

She was as nervous as he seemed confident and pulled her hand away from his. Paul smiled as she laid both hands on her lap. Meredith wasn't sure what was happening between the pair of old friends, but to her, everything seemed to be moving too quickly. It felt as if Paul was hinting for more.

She took a deep breath and began to speak just as her cell phone rang. Recognizing the number, she excused herself and spoke for a minute but didn't take time to explain to the caller where she was or who she was with. There would be time for that when they met at the San Diego Airport.

Upon hanging up, she told Paul it was her eldest daughter, Jennifer, checking on her. "She still thinks I shouldn't be traveling alone and likes to keep track of me. It often seems as if our mother-daughter roles have reversed. She acts as if I am incapable of looking after myself."

Paul smiled. "Can you?" he asked.

"Of course I can," she replied. "But with so much going on in the world today one can't be too careful. Since Alex died, the only traveling I have done is to visit Stephen and his family in England, and Claire and Heather Ann in New York City. Coming to Washington, DC, by myself was a big step."

"I am glad you took that step," Paul said. Again, he had an uncontrollable urge to reach for Meredith's hand, but he held back.

"I have been alone since Rachel died except for novelty women, as I call them. It was difficult for me to date. I always felt dating was for teenagers."

"I'm not sure there is a place for me in the dating world," Meredith replied, "and at my age, I can't think of anything more unsettling."

Meredith felt more comfortable with Paul since he had given her a glimpse into his past. Now it was her turn to bring the conversation back to the last forty-plus years, but would he think her life dull even though by most standards it had been full and exciting? Business, though not the scope of Paul's, had been a large part of her life. Travel, children, and lifelong friends weren't multiple offices worldwide, but they were her world.

Her mind was suddenly in another place and time. Was it staring into his eyes across the table that made her remember the past so clearly?

She was outside her apartment in Phoenix watching Stephen and Jennifer play. She had just told the children it was dinner time when a construction truck pulled up nearby. She froze in place as she stared into the face of Paul Richardson, her old college flame. As their eyes met, he too had looked stunned. He gazed down her slim body to the hands that held her two small children as he stepped from the truck cabin.

It had been five years since college, and their last farewell on the river's edge, and his *I love you* came into her mind. She closed her eyes to blot out the memory.

Upon opening them, she found herself staring once again into the dark pool of Paul's brown eyes.

After what seemed like minutes, Meredith extended her hand to Paul, and he held it in his.

"Great to see you again," he blurted out as he also tried to stay calm. He noticed the plain silver band on her left hand, and she tried to be nonchalant about noticing his wedding band.

She told Paul of her husband Alex, her children Stephen and Jennifer, and tried to act like a grown-up married woman.

Meredith wondered what his wife was like. He was a wonderful person with high ideals and deserved to be loved in a way she had not been able to do. He had aged well, filled out, and was more handsome than in his football years. His thick brown hair seemed fuller, his waist slimmer, and his shoulders broader.

She wondered what he was thinking and she snapped herself back to reality and politely inquired about his life. Did he have children? How was his mother, who she had always loved, and how did he come to be driving a construction truck down her street, so near her house and so close to her heart?

Yes, he was married and had two sons, ages three and four. He worked in construction, as she would have predicted, had married a girl from the neighborhood, and was content. At least he had been until this moment he realized.

Their eyes met and she wondered what *their* children might have looked like had they remained together. Dark skin and dark eyes, she imagined.

Stephen tugged on his mother's hand to draw her from her trance. This chance meeting with Paul had an astonishing effect on her, and she needed to pull herself together, return her thoughts to her family, and stop the old memories of him. It was time to cook dinner for her family.

As he said goodbye and turned to climb into the cab of his large truck, she felt strange. Would she see him again? Does the experience of first love ever leave you or is it a special memory you store forever in the far corners of your mind? He waved another quick goodbye and drove off.

Through the kitchen window, she saw him drive past her complex a few days later and forced herself to turn away. But that did not explain her curiosity, and why every few days she looked out that window at the same time of day hoping to catch a glimpse of him.

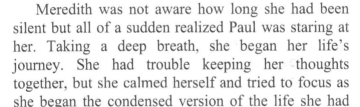

Meredith was not aware how long she had been silent but all of a sudden realized Paul was staring at her. Taking a deep breath, she began her life's journey. She had trouble keeping her thoughts together, but she calmed herself and tried to focus as she began the condensed version of the life she had shared with Alex.

Starting with her three children, she told him of their early move to California, of Alex's success as the owner of a golf course architecture and construction firm, and her years of owning three retail gift businesses in the exclusive communities of Palm Springs and Las Vegas. She then quickly added shortened versions of family marriages and divorces and ended by telling him of Alex's tragic death.

The dark eyes across the table saddened as she

spoke of Alex. As if she knew what had been on both their minds, she blurted out in a very matter-of-fact voice, "We did the honorable thing all those years ago. What we were contemplating would have ruined so many lives."

Paul nodded in agreement but still felt the pain of the truth.

Meredith knew she had been right in not taking that step with Paul and she was grateful not to have destroyed her husband's happiness. She assured Paul what happened that day on the riverbank had been forgotten, at least until today.

Now here they sat, so many years later, across the table from each other and both unattached.

Meredith happened to glance at her watch and realized time was catching up with them. "I need to check in for my flight," she said. But there was more to be said, and she couldn't believe the words coming from her lips. "Maybe we can continue this another time," she added.

"Will there be another time?" he questioned.

Her response was interrupted by the waiter who laid the leather-bound bill holder beside Paul. He opened it to insert his Platinum American Express card and suddenly had a look of surprise on his face. Their lunch had already been taken care of. The folder contained a note from Karen saying she hoped they enjoyed their time with each other. She also included a special note for Meredith telling her how delightful their visit had been and offering wishes for a safe trip home.

Paul drew a business card from a small elegant case and passed it to Meredith. "Just in case you misplaced the one I gave you last night, here are my private phone numbers. My executive assistant, Mrs. Parker, knows how to reach me at all times. I think you also sense something has brought us together. I would like to see you again, but it's your turn this time, Meredith. The ball is in your court." With a small smile, he continued, "I am too old to handle much rejection, so the next move is up to you."

"I guess I deserve that after our last meeting," she answered. "Thank you for the delicious lunch and your phone numbers. I will call you."

Meredith felt like a schoolgirl gathering her books, but this time it was her carry-on bag. Paul considered reaching for her hand but chose not to and rose with her as they stood to leave. Taking a step, she faltered, and thinking she might fall, he reached for her arm. For a moment he cushioned her against him. Suddenly, they were alone on the dusty road at the river's edge, except he was older and wiser and determined not to show emotion.

He stepped away and said, "You travel light," as he released her arm.

"Years of practice and organization," she replied, as she turned to leave.

Exiting the restaurant, they walked across the hall to the elevator and stood looking at each other. "Let's part here," Meredith said. "I am used to being dropped off places and the hotel will get me to the airport terminal." But Paul insisted on helping her pick up the bags and walking Meredith to her car.

As the elevator doors opened, little did they know within a few short months they would wish they owned stock in Otis Elevator Company.

Exiting the elevator, they walked side by side to the counter for her bags, neither looking at the other, nor speaking, alone with their thoughts. They approached the waiting airport limo, each knowing the meaning of airport hellos and goodbyes, and handed her luggage over to the driver. "It's been wonderful seeing you again, Paul," she said softly as she leaned against his shoulder. She thought she heard him whisper *don't leave me again* but on the busy DC street, his words were muffled and may have been only wishful thinking on her part.

He lifted her face, and with a strong smile leaned to kiss her goodbye on the cheek. As he did, he added, "Think about me and call when you can."

The driver stood at the open car door, and Paul helped her into the rear seat. As the car pulled away, Meredith turned to look through the window for a final glance at him, just as she had done forty years before.

I will see you again Meredith Jamison Evans, he almost said aloud. I won't let you get away again, but the next move is yours. A little later than planned, but somehow we will have our time together.

CHAPTER 6

The ride to Reagan National Airport was brief and Meredith was pleased there was no line at the United Airlines ticket counter. A miracle, she thought. Soon she was on her way to gate twenty-eight where she found a seat near the window in the waiting area. She opened her book to read but couldn't concentrate. Lunch was all she could think about. Lunch with a handsome man who had once said he loved her.

Within a few minutes, her flight was called, and she located her seat in row eight. After she stowed her small carry-on bag under the seat in front of her, she gazed out the window. Remembering Karen's *you never know who you may meet* comment, she thought again about her unexpected reconnection with Paul and wondered where might it lead.

When all the passengers were settled, the pilot announced they were third in line for takeoff. They began to taxi down the very long runway and soon they were soaring into the sky. Meredith took one last look at the beautiful skyline of DC, wondering if Paul was standing at a window thinking of her.

He was probably already rushing to attend an important business meeting. But he had kissed her goodbye. It was a pleasant sort of goodbye kiss—the kind you might give a friend. Why was she still thinking of it, she wondered, as she raised her hand to touch the cheek he had kissed.

Meredith couldn't help analyzing the events of the last five days, something her family told her was her real claim to fame. She decided seeing Karen should have been enough excitement, but running into Paul after all these years, was almost unbelievable. Nothing could have prepared her for that unexpected surprise, but would she ever see him again?

As the plane moved through the brilliant blue sky Meredith treated herself to a glass of her favorite white wine. It was a four and a half hour flight, and when she finished her wine she adjusted her seat and drifted off to sleep, dreaming of the handsome man she had lunch with and who had surprised her with a kiss goodbye. It had been a long time since a man kissed her, even on the cheek, and her mind began to wander back to that day on the riverbank so long ago.

Alex was asked to supervise a night shift for an I-10 freeway expansion project. His late hours meant more sleeping in the daytime and she was forced out of their small apartment to keep the two active children quiet. So off they would go to the pool each afternoon.

Glancing around the area after she helped the children into the water, she was surprised to see Paul again, standing very near and staring at the cleavage of her swimsuit. She greeted him with a cautious smile as she played with Stephen and Jennifer in the pool. Although both of them loved the water, neither could properly swim yet so it was a full-time job keeping the two active toddlers safe. Paul pulled a patio chair up near the edge of the pool and watched the way mother and son splashed together as she also kept a close eye on the younger Jennifer.

Why was he here, she wondered. His wife was probably home preparing dinner for their family and yet here he sat eyeing his old girlfriend.

Their conversation was simple and polite at first, but before she realized what was happening, she felt like a college girl again, laughing with the popular football jock.

Then he reached out and touched her hand.

Suddenly apprehensive and uncomfortable with the way Paul was watching her, she made excuses that it was time for the children's naps as she gathered Jennifer and Stephen to her. As they all got out of the pool, Paul stood and reached for Meredith's hand to help her, a gesture she felt too personal. Again, their eyes met, and the lust in his eyes was inescapable. Meredith reached for a towel to dry Jennifer off. Anticipating her need, he covered her with the dry towel lying on a chair.

As his arms came around her, she could not help but feel a sense of excitement. He took the liberty of brushing her cheek. It seemed a casual gesture but it felt like fire, and she knew the sensible thing to do was to put it out. They stood inches from each other, neither knowing what might come next.

Feeling the need to be safe inside her home, Meredith said a hasty goodbye, took the children's hands, and walked quickly towards her apartment, careful to not look back.

When Meredith had the children changed and

tucked in for their naps, she ventured into her tiny bathroom and stared into the mirror. Who was this woman? What was she thinking—letting another man touch her?

Later that night the phone rang, and she hurried to answer so the noise would not wake the children. She stated her *hello* barely above a whisper.

It was Paul calling from a payphone. She clutched the phone to her ear for fear his words would escape into the room. He pleaded with her to see him just once. Could they meet and just talk, and he would never bother her again? She was afraid to speak and would have hung up but was sure he would call back.

After his final plea and her shaky, non-committal response, she quietly placed the receiver back on the cradle and prayed he would never call again.

Meredith was awakened from her dream when the seats in her row were nudged by the stewardess pushing her drink cart. She couldn't believe she was able to remember all the details from so many years ago. The children always said she had the worst memory of anyone they knew. Why were these all so vivid?

She contemplated having a second cocktail but thought better of it, then changed her mind. What harm could another glass of wine do?

She refused the snack as she and Jennifer had their ritual of meeting at the airport and going straight to their favorite dockside eatery. Who had the best clam chowder in all of San Diego? Well, Sam's on the Pier, of course. What would she do without the memories of all the wonderful family times spent on the waterfront and what would she tell her daughter about running into Paul again after so many years? She smiled when she realized she had another two hours before she would meet the family whirlwind at baggage claim.

Sleep or dream? She chose to dream.

Drowsy from the second glass of wine she let herself drift back to their last meeting on the riverbank.

The following week Alex announced the freeway project was moving slower than expected and he was tasked with two extra weekend night shifts. He suggested Meredith and the kids spend the time with her parents. She reluctantly agreed. She knew she would feel safer from Paul at her parents' home and it would be a good place to hide. Deep down she didn't trust herself to say no if Paul called again and she was alone. What was she thinking? It was over, and he wasn't going to call. Things like that only happen in the movies.

Friday afternoon, Meredith packed the children into the back seat of the family car and was turning out of the complex parking lot when she saw Paul's familiar truck down the street pulled off to the side of the road. As her car reached his truck she slowed, grateful her children, just two and three, were too young to pass on any words spoken between herself and Paul. She stopped, rolled down her car window, and said, "Hello." Paul replied with a warm smile, the one she was remembering all too well these days.

He asked her where she was going, and she responded, "My parent's home for a quick visit."

"Could you please meet me for a few minutes later today at the river's edge?" She started to protest, but he pleaded with her and told her how much he needed to talk to her. "I'll be there at six o'clock and will wait for you. Please, just come this one time. I'll wait," he repeated.

Meredith knew it was wrong and didn't say yes. She simply rolled up the car window and drove away not knowing how to respond but not having the courage to say no.

The river's edge was the place where they had spent so many hours in each other's arms, and she knew they couldn't be seen. As she drove to her parent's home on the east side of Phoenix, Meredith knew this situation had to be put to rest. She needed to get him out of her life and back to his wife and family. Seeing him was dangerous.

Meredith lied to her parents and told them she was going shopping for a couple of hours. Then she kissed the children and drove off to meet Paul.

Was she out of her mind to jeopardize everything to see a man who had once told her he loved her? Would one last time put the situation to rest or would it wake up the feelings she had for him so many years ago? Why did she feel she owed him one last meeting and a real goodbye?

Driving down the secluded road, her pulse raced. She didn't know what to expect. Maybe he wouldn't even be there but as she rounded the all too familiar bend in the road, she saw him standing beside his truck waiting for her. Meredith stopped her car near him. She reached for the door, but he was quicker and opened it for her, extending his hand to help her exit.

Afraid to touch him, she refused his outstretched hand, but got out of the car and stood leaning against the door to steady herself. He didn't move toward her. They stood a few feet apart. Who would make the first move?

"Thanks for coming," Paul said.

"I can't stay long," she replied. "I feel guilty even being here. I have never lied to my parents this way, and I need to get right back." She looked down at her feet as if willing them back into the car.

At that moment, Paul reached his hand to her chin and raised her face to his. Before either of them knew what was happening, his lips came down gently on hers as if to kiss away the guilt.

Meredith tried to back away, but his kiss was so affectionate she was drawn into him. Her hands came to rest on his strong forearms. When he whispered her name, it brought back memories she thought had vanished. She opened her eyes half expecting to see Alex, but there stood Paul. She could not get over the urge to have his hands on her body.

Paul looked into her eyes and began kissing her harder until his lips forced her mouth open. Her entire body was shaking and she felt him move closer. As if they had a mind of their own, her arms reached higher and joined at the nape of his strong neck, and she was soon recalling the feel of his neck, his body, and, oh! his mouth.

Meredith also remembered their sudden parting, each knowing where another kiss would lead them. If they kept kissing like this they would soon be making love. She knew if they stopped now, they would never know what might have been, but if they continued it would bring them physical pleasure and disastrous results to their two families.

Suddenly awakened by the voice of the captain, she couldn't stop clutching at those vivid memories and searched her thoughts for what else had happened that afternoon. But they were landing in the beautiful city she loved and called home, San Diego.

Her dreams would have to wait. With tray tables put away and her seat in the *upright and locked position,* she began gathering her belongings for landing. She would tuck her memories away for now.

Exiting the plane, she hurried up the jetway and down the short walk to the baggage claim area. There, talking on her cell phone, as usual, was her tall, elegant daughter. Meredith rushed to greet her best friend and confidante, her wonderful Jennifer.

CHAPTER 7

Paul had to control himself from sliding into the back seat of the car next to Meredith, but this time, he decided, she would have to want him there. Yes, he was older, but he still loved life and had much to offer the right person.

Meredith had no idea of the extent of his wealth and power, and he intended to keep it that way. Too many women recognized the RCC logo and came scratching for all he had. Little did they know he would give it all to the right woman.

He stood at the busy entrance to the Hyatt Hotel knowing his driver, Jake, was waiting for his sign a few yards away. Paul flagged him down and, stepping into the rear seat, was torn between thoughts of business and the pleasure he wanted to experience with Meredith.

As they drove through the congested traffic, he watched a plane take off, his thoughts full of Meredith with the hope she was thinking of him too. The ride to his office building should be brief but sitting in the snarled DC traffic he knew it would take longer than usual to drive down Pennsylvania Avenue. As much as he tried to keep his mind on his upcoming business meeting, he was lulled into remembering the last afternoon spent with Meredith at the river's edge.

Paul had begged Meredith earlier in the day to meet him at their private place but was not at all sure if she would show up. Regardless, he would wait, all night if necessary.

He had lied to his wife about a business meeting and promised to call her if he would be too late. (Then he remembered there were no cell phones in those days. Quarters and public payphones were all that were available. He smiled thinking just how far the world had come.)

When he saw Meredith's car round the bend, his heart leaped in his chest. He remembered trying to help her from the car and her refusal of his hand.

He also recalled that first kiss. Just one touch, he told himself, and he would send her home. Home to her husband and children, but he knew deep down one kiss would never be enough. How he wanted her that evening on the riverbank, more than at the age of twenty. He knew much more about love. He had always thought himself a good lover, but was he better than her husband? Did that matter and did he even care?

Their lives had taken separate paths and now they were alone on a dusty road not knowing what lay ahead. His guilt was as overwhelming as his desire. But when she raised her eyes to his, the battle was lost and his mind told him she was his real love.

His arms slid around her back and pulled her close. He couldn't think straight, for if he did, he would release her and he had her now, close, nestled in his arms. It was as if their bodies had been connected for years. His firm hands caressed her back and moved down to force her closer at the same moment his mouth claimed hers.

Meredith clung to him, and her small hands crept uncontrollably up his arms. She felt his ears, his cheeks, and the back of his neck. Every touch sent him further into her mouth with his tongue doing what the rest of his body was craving. He couldn't stop himself, and when he felt her small hands on his shoulders pulling him into her, all reason seemed lost.

Meredith didn't want to stop any more than he did. His hands roamed under her blouse and were moving to unfasten her bra. It happened so fast, and then those beautiful breasts he had admired at the pool were in his hands. She let out a soft sound. Her nipples hardened at his touch and were their own response. She didn't resist.

He remembered not trying to remove the blouse but rather pushed it aside to frame the photo of her in his mind. She did not resist as he bent his head to suck first one breast and then the other. Meredith's legs began to crumble.

They both felt exposed, and it made the experience more exciting than either could have anticipated. "Make love with me, Meredith," he heard himself say.

He should not have paused in his pursuit of her because at that moment she pulled away and with shaky hands closed her blouse and stared into his eyes.

"This is wrong, Paul, and we both know it."

And knowing she was right made him want her more. Did he love her or was it just lustful desire? He thought she cared for him or she would never have come, but was this their last goodbye? He had felt her excitement, touched her, but she belonged to Alex Evans and he was married to Rachel. By the look on Meredith's face, Paul knew this stolen meeting was all they would ever have together.

Meredith looked into his eyes. "I will never forget you and for a brief instance, we shared something romantic and exciting. But our families need us, and we must do the right thing. We couldn't live with ourselves if we took this any further, and we both know it."

He would always remember her adding *thank you for wanting me*. Holding her unbuttoned blouse together and on shaky legs, she entered her car, closed the door, and quickly drove away.

He could only stare as his dream disappeared.

Paul closed his eyes and laid his head back on the seat of his town car. He could still see her that day on the river's edge. He had wanted to race after her, but they had done the right thing. An affair with Meredith would have destroyed both their lives.

Their paths had crossed for a brief encounter. They were young and in love for a moment, but it was over. He had promised himself he would forget Meredith and become a loving father to the boys and a faithful husband to Rachel.

Meredith had always seemed like a fairy princess to him. She was reared in a good religious home where he was always made to feel welcome. He was Hispanic on his mother's side and his father was of English descent. He was a straight-A student and captain of the college football team but felt her parents believed he would never amount to anything and never really be successful.

What would her family think now of his lavish lifestyle, private jets, and high government contacts? Add to that his secret ties to the White House.

He could certainly show them how successful Paul Richardson had become.

Just then the car jolted in traffic and Paul realized he had almost dozed off. A smile crossed his face as he recognized his approaching office. Success does strange things to people, he thought, and as the car came to a stop, he was once again back in control.

He would set aside his thoughts of Meredith and take on the United States Government, at least for now.

CHAPTER 8

Jennifer and Meredith embraced at the baggage claim carousel. "Mother, you look wonderful," she said with a smile. "DC must have agreed with you."

As they picked up her rolling bags, Meredith said, "I'll tell you all about it at dinner." They walked to her car and of course, it was the newest and fastest one in the lot. They drove out Harbor Drive towards downtown through light traffic. They arrived at Sam's on the Pier ordered their favorites, clam chowder, French bread, and shared an order of the best fish and chips in all San Diego.

Meredith began by telling Jen about all the sightseeing, visiting Karen's very important office, dinner parties, and shopping. She casually mentioned meeting her old friend, Paul Richardson. She skimmed over their reunion but couldn't bring herself to tell her most worldly daughter she had met an old beau who had even kissed her goodbye.

Tired from her long day and even longer flight, and relaxed after two glasses of wine, Meredith was eager to get home to her condo and unpack. Jennifer paid the check, and they were soon on their way to Coronado.

Meredith always loved returning to The Shores.

The physical size of the buildings never ceased to amaze her. There are ten buildings at the complex but only three faced the ocean. Meredith and Alex had always preferred the bayside and were fortunate to have found a corner unit with a large wrap-around patio which gave them both an ocean and bay view. The lights of downtown San Diego made her feel part of a big city, which was a stark contrast to the dark side of the ocean. Meredith enjoyed spending evenings on the patio looking at the beautiful waves lit by large floodlights of the buildings. The sparkling city lights across the Bay Bridge dazzled in the moonlight, and the sound of her jagged waves would soon be music to her ears.

"This is the most wonderful place on earth," she said as Jen turned onto Orange Avenue.

"I know how much you love it here, Mom, and I can only imagine how hard it is for you to be alone. I'm glad you are comfortable and secure, and we don't have to worry about your safety."

But what would Jennifer think if she knew someone once close to her was out to destroy their entire family? How could she protect her mother from the unknown dangers that lay ahead? Dangers primarily caused by her wild way of life.

Their oldest daughter Jennifer Evans Sanders, whose surname came from Jeffery, ex-husband number two, visited Meredith often.

As much as Meredith loved Jen, she knew her daughter had a wild side. When Jen ran away to marry Dave Andres, a wanna-be baseball player after her first semester in college, Meredith and Alex were devasted. But Dave had convinced her he had what it took to make it in the big leagues and she was in love with both him and the idea of being a major league ballplayer's wife.

Time spent in the minors for all young baseball players was a wild ride. Of course, no one had any money, and during the season as Dave traveled from town to town on the team bus, Jennifer was stuck with the other player's wives in whatever backwater town Dave happened to be playing in. There was always a party going on and Dave was on a fast climb up the farm team ladders.

After three years of minor league ball, he got a call from the majors when a team was trying out new talent for the upcoming year. It seemed he was finally going to make good on the promise he made to Jennifer when they married.

However, the spark he showed on minor league fields failed to ignite in the big league. His bat went cold and too many fielding errors had his number next to them in the record book. As his popularity began to shift so did his habits and soon they involved the use of drugs. If the team went into a slump or he was sidelined by injury, his drug use became worse. After two warnings from team management, he was fired.

He began taking out his frustrations on Jennifer and once in a wild rage almost beat her unconscious. Devastated and defeated, she called her parents. Alex picked her up and brought her home to heal. A quiet divorce followed.

Meredith tried to help her daughter, but she and her co-owner, Stacy, were busy getting their new retail store up and running. After a discussion with Stacy and Alex, they offered Jen a trial period to work for them as a bookkeeper. She was excellent with numbers, but there remained a question as to whether she would apply herself working for her mother in the family business.

It turned out to be the right decision and as the old saying goes *the rest is history*. Twenty-five years later she was beyond successful and Meredith now considered her daughter "the boss." She was the proud owner of two retail stores in the Palm Springs area and was considering franchising into Northern California. She drove fast and lived fast, that was always her style.

Jeffery Sanders met Jennifer at a dance club in the early '90s. Soon it was strawberries and whipped cream and a wild courtship they both enjoyed. They married in grand style in a whirlwind ceremony over three days in Las Vegas. Although the Evans family seemed to care for him, he was never sure he fit the mold of the perfect son-in-law for their precious Jen.

He had grown up in a bad part of Los Angeles and was determined to get out of the city and make something of himself. He studied to be an electrician at a local vocational center and then moved to the desert to earn his residential electrician license. In between the hours required to train for his chosen career, Jeff played golf, was great fun at a dinner party, and had the fastest boat on the lake. He was a social guy and could schmooze with the best and wealthiest in the desert.

Once he received his license, Jen set him up in his own electrical contracting business. Between her connections and the rapid growth in the desert, he was an overnight success. But within three years, he was cheating on Jennifer and neglecting the business. Soon he started going out nights with the boys and Jen knew it was over.

Their divorce was messy. It was a big scandal that rocked their small town as everyone knew her. Jeff always smiled at the thought of the embarrassment she must be experiencing.

Jen paid for the divorce and bought him out of any investments they had shared. He took the money, of course, and almost immediately remarried. But within a year the money was gone and so was the new wife. He was deep in debt again and banged around from job to job. When her lawyer told him he would not get another cent from Jennifer or her family he vowed to ruin them all.

Jeff had always secretly envied Meredith and Alex for their success, but most of all he was jealous of the love the family shared. His own family was never close and barely scraped by.

He refused to take responsibility for his mistakes and slipped lower and lower, finally ending up back in downtown LA, living in a one-room hostel doing drugs with his fellow suitemates. He brought drugs up to LA from San Diego and began dealing whatever he didn't snort.

When he was lucid, his thoughts always returned to the Evans family. They had introduced him to the lifestyle he always wanted, but when things didn't work out they dumped him like they would the daily garbage.

Well, Jeff was determined to make sure they never forgot him again and hoped his plans would ruin all of their lives in the process.

Jen's second failed marriage left her bitter about men and money. *I will never support another man* became her motto during the nineties. She was successful beyond her wildest dreams in business, but a failure with every man she met until Stanley Barrington, a local banker.

They met through mutual friends and were extremely well suited for each other. Her connection to anyone of importance made Jennifer and Stan an unbeatable pair He was rich, powerful, and although years her senior, looked younger than his sixty years. Best of all, Meredith knew he was head and shoulders above all the Tom, Dick, and Harry's Jennifer had slept with over the years.

Jennifer became the consummate hostess for all Stan's social and business functions. She traveled to his San Francisco home when she could and even took up golf, a sport she swore she would never play, but it was Stan's favorite. She was mellowing and trying to fit into his world.

While in the desert, they resided at the prestigious Verrado Country Club in the exclusive desert city of Indian Wells. It was an old club with even older money and his family's fifth-generation San Francisco roots fit right in. Although no marriage plans were imminent, they lived together in his small, but adequate sixty-two hundred square foot home with perfectly manicured lawns and gardens, overlooking the eighteenth green of the club's golf course.

Jennifer called her mother every day, sometimes two or three times, to make sure she was safe and sane. Meredith was beginning to feel she was the child and Jen, Meredith's favorite nickname for her, the mother.

Down deep Meredith felt a twinge of envy at the exciting lifestyle Jennifer led, but she wished her all the happiness in the world. Jen had paid her dues and earned every wonderful thing she now enjoyed. She was allowing herself to be engulfed by Stan, his love, and his business. It was her time, and she was living life to the fullest.

They entered the living room and walked to the large sliding glass door of the patio. "Welcome home, Mom," Jennifer said as she put her arms around her. "I'm glad you had such a wonderful trip."

Meredith kissed her daughter, "I definitely did. Spending time with Karen again was such fun and running into my old friend, Paul, was a wonderful surprise. Thanks again for the prompt airport pickup and dinner. If you don't mind though, I'm on East Coast time and I'm so tired. I'm going to bed early tonight." They decided to call it an evening and headed to their bedrooms, leaving the drapes open, knowing the warm sun would wake them in the morning. Crawling under the covers Meredith felt a sudden chill. If only there was someone to keep her warm.

She woke the next morning after a long, deep sleep to the aroma of freshly brewed coffee. It had taken Jennifer twenty years to begin drinking coffee, but when she did, it was with gusto as she did everything in life. It was too cool for breakfast on the patio, so they sat curled up on the couch looking more like sisters than mother and daughter.

They spent an hour catching up on Jen's stores and her busy life with Stan. They laughed about customers, young and old, and discussed new merchandising ideas Jen had for next season. She was lucky to have the cream of desert dwellers as her customer base. Meredith was always pleased when Jennifer asked her opinion of new product lines as it made her feel she was still a part of the business she would always love.

Meredith was so proud of the life Jen had made for herself in the resort town she had finally come to love and call home. She remembered how, as a young woman, Jennifer had dreaded moving to the small desert community she referred to as *retirement central*.

Between two retail businesses and living with Stan, Jennifer had little spare time but somehow she always found time for girl talks with mom, something Claire was too private to do. Jennifer didn't seem interested in marriage and when asked she would laughingly say, "You don't have to be married in today's world."

Meredith always felt it was a cover-up for all the feelings Jennifer kept secret in her heart. She would use her favorite *it works for me* argument when describing situations, both in work and her private life, and as the two women talked, it was as if time stood still.

Meredith's mind passed from Jen to Alex. He sometimes felt like an outsider when the two were in their mother-daughter mode, never quite understanding the bond the two women shared. Some days they would disagree, followed by days of love and joy. *That's how mothers and daughters are* Meredith would say.

Too soon Jennifer announced she had to be at a dinner party with Stan at six and by noon kissed her mom goodbye and left to drive back to the desert.

Meredith settled into reorganizing her so-called orderly life. Mundane tasks such as laundry were done and suitcases stashed, a duty previously delegated to Alex. Finally, she sat down to read the mail.

Although Meredith loved receiving emails, she always sent handwritten notes to her many friends and the thought reminded her to drop a line to Karen and thank her for the wonderful time spent together in DC, and for the lunch she had shared with Paul.

She stood for a while watching the rolling waves splash towards the shore. *Where had they been?* she wondered. They come and go at a whim as the world stands still. As she watched the waves, Meredith wondered just where her life was headed.

The next morning, feeling rested, Meredith dressed in her usual fleece-lined sweats and tennis shoes and took off for her beach walk. The gold whistle she wore around her neck was her constant reminder Alex always wanted her to be safe. Had she noticed the person lurking in the shadows of her building, she would not have been so sure of her safety and confident in her surroundings. Jeffery Sanders had followed her down the boardwalk many times and gone completely unnoticed. He was putting his plan of revenge in place.

By mid-week, her life was back to normal and time to think came all too often. More than once she walked to the phone and checked her messages in hopes Paul might have called. But he had made it clear the next step was hers. She made excuses to herself all week guessing how busy he must be, and even if she did call was sure he would not have time to speak to her.

When Friday brought little hope for anything but another long weekend alone, she gave in, picked up the business card that had been lying beside her bedroom telephone all week, and dialed the first of the five numbers on Paul's card.

A strong woman's voice answered. "Paul Richardson's private line. May I help you?"

Meredith paused, took a deep breath, and announced, "Meredith Evans calling for Mr. Richardson."

"One moment please," the woman replied, and within a few seconds, Meredith heard Paul's voice on the line.

"Did you have a good trip home?" he inquired in a very matter-of-fact voice.

Meredith was quick to respond yes and say how sorry she was for not calling sooner to thank him for taking time to lunch with her.

"Where are you?" she asked.

"My London office," Paul replied. "I flew here as soon as my DC meetings were over. Are you up for dinner tomorrow night?" he asked.

"But you're in London," she replied.

"I will be back in San Diego by 4 p.m. tomorrow and can pick you up at 7:30."

Her mind raced. Don't think, just say yes, and she did.

She started to give him directions and was interrupted. "Mrs. Parker will have all I need. See you at 7:30," and after a quick goodbye was off the line.

Meredith stared in disbelief at the phone in her hand. Just who was Paul Richardson, and how would his Mrs. Parker know where she lived?

She counted the hours from London to San Diego and decided it would be possible, although he would probably have to fly all night. She was bound and determined to find out more about him at dinner tomorrow evening.

Then panic set in. Where were they going and what should she wear? But the concern and questions were quickly set aside as she thought of what she always said to her children in stressful situations— *I will think about that tomorrow,* just like Miss Scarlett, and she trotted off to prepare her dinner.

The corner of the patio sheltered her from the

ocean breezes and she pondered her upcoming evening. She needed to stay calm, set thoughts of Paul aside, get to bed early, and finish the book she had carried to DC and back.

Later that evening, Meredith smiled to herself as she undressed. All her life she had worn beautiful lingerie and her family called her their Loretta Young. She loved silky gowns that flowed when she walked. Alex never reached and found flannel in forty years of marriage, and she swore flannel was the cause of many divorces.

Lulled to sleep by the sound of her jagged waves, Meredith woke around two a.m. thinking she heard a noise. She got up. The night chill caused her to shudder, and she reached for her robe. After searching through the condo and finding no reason for concern, she went back to bed and was once again remembering Paul and their goodbye on the river's edge.

She had been deep in thought as her car pulled away that night to return to her parents' house. She kept repeating to herself, *I have done the right thing. I have done the right thing.* She entered the house quietly as to not wake any of the family and checked on the children asleep in their cribs.

Paul had put his hands on her body, and that thought would not leave her mind. He had taken the liberty of touching her, and her name had come as a prayer on his lips.

But Paul was married. She was married and to the most wonderful, loving, and exciting man in the world. There should be no other man for her, and at that moment she made her decision. She would raise her children and be a devoted wife to Alex. They would be a picture-perfect family. She would make sure of it and never see Paul Richardson again. What they had shared that night on the river's edge was now forever stored in her book of memories.

Had their recent reunion found the key to unlock that special place?

Meredith woke to the ringing of her telephone. Still drowsy, but thinking it might be Paul and that he had changed his mind, she reached for the receiver. But it was Claire calling from New York along with a, "Sorry Mom, did I wake you?"

They chatted about her trip to DC and Claire shared a few details about some of the interesting cases she was working on. Then they moved to the one thing they had most in common—Heather Ann and her latest A+ homework successes. Meredith wanted to speak to her granddaughter, but she was out with friends. Claire could hear the disappointment in her mother's voice.

Their conversation was brief as usual and Claire encouraged her to visit again soon and Meredith promised to try. Why was it nothing ever happened to bring them closer together?

Meredith climbed out of bed and headed for the kitchen. She needed her morning coffee and it was a beautiful September day on the beach. Coffee in hand, she walked to the patio to enjoy the view. After sitting for a few minutes, the details of the day came alive in her head. Heavens, she thought, he'll be here at 7:30.

Meredith was a young sixty-something when Alex was taken from her. She was smart and bright, an excellent businesswoman, and still felt fun-loving, and vibrant. From the moment she and Alex made their first home in San Diego where he had been stationed as a US Navy sailor, Meredith considered herself a California girl. As she rubbed lotion on her legs, she thought of the times she had promised herself to start going to the gym, but her California blonde hair gave her the best appearance she could hope for. After all, as people say, age is just a number.

The day passed quickly and soon it was time to get ready for her first important date in over forty years. She had no idea what to wear as she didn't know where they were going. She looked through her closet full of beach clothes and after considerable deliberation decided on a pale green cashmere sweater set and white knit pants. She added her signature touch of matching white socks, as her feet were always cold, and then went in search of the right pair of shoes. Paul was not as tall as Alex, so she chose flats to appear a bit shorter next to him. Would she even get next to him? The thought made her smile.

Meredith glanced down at her wedding ring now worn on her right hand. She had faced such loneliness, but tonight she was looking forward to a special evening with an old friend.

She slid three etched gold bracelets on her wrist and her favorite strand of pearls around her neck then turned to take a long hard look in the mirror. Thinking the pearls looked a bit dated, she put them back in their case and reached for a gold Omega necklace instead. A little glamour never hurt a girl.

Suddenly doubts began creeping in. Should she call Paul and cancel this so-called date? What business did she have sitting in front of a mirror applying makeup and choosing jewelry for anyone other than Alex?

A cloud suddenly shadowed the beach. Was this Alex telling her don't go, you're mine, or was he giving her his blessing? When a streak of sunlight appeared through the cloud, she had her answer.

Meredith recalled a conversation she and Alex had shared years before—an *if I die before you* conversation. She knew he didn't want her to hide away and grieve him for the rest of her life.

She felt sure she could handle one dinner with an old friend.

CHAPTER 9

The sun was just beginning to set as she prepared a tray of gin and tonic. She had called the doorman and he seemed happy Mrs. Evans was having a gentleman caller. When her doorbell rang, she checked her hair in the hall mirror and opened the door.

Paul looked so handsome, as she had expected. He was dressed smartly in a beautiful gray mock turtleneck sweater, charcoal slacks, and a black blazer. He looked every bit the dashing man he now was. Black was definitely his color.

"Come in," she said as she reached to shake his hand. "Welcome to my home."

"It's just what I imagined," he replied, and in what seemed like four giant John Wayne strides, walked to the large open patio doors. "I have always loved the beach, but never taken time to enjoy it."

Meredith smiled and laughingly said, "My children call me the oldest beach bum in California. Our family has always loved the beach, and I walk it every day."

"I am too busy to do much but walk from one project or airport to another," he said. "A week here would be heaven."

Was he asking for a week here, she wondered? Paul glanced to see Meredith's reaction. There was no invitation pouring from her lips, which was the reaction he had expected. In Meredith's mind, she was wondering if he was waiting for one. Well, he won't get one from me, and certainly not on the first date.

Paul resisted the urge to take the four steps back and take Meredith in his arms.

Meredith played at being the gracious hostess and tried making him a drink, but Paul was quick to take over the task. "It was never in my job description," she said with a laugh, as they walked onto the terrace.

After a bit more polite conversation on the patio and knowing what a second drink would do to her, Meredith suggested they go to dinner.

"With your long trip, you must be suffering from a bit of jet lag and may want to call it an early night." She had no idea he had flown back from London on his own 737 corporate jet complete with bedroom, living room, and full staff. He had spent a couple of hours catching up on work and then was able to enjoy a good night's sleep soaring through the skies dreaming of his first date with Meredith since his college days over forty years ago.

"Where are we dining?" she asked.

"One of my favorite San Diego restaurants," he replied. Paul seemed to be implying he came to town often and he was letting her know he was familiar with her city. Well, she doubted that.

He suggested she take a wrap. "It's quite cool outside unless, of course, you want me to keep you warm."

Meredith couldn't help but imagine how it would feel to have a man's arms around her again but agreed and walked to the bedroom for her favorite long white coat. Paul reached to help her and caught a whiff of her perfume. "You smell delicious," he whispered in her ear, as they turned to the door. Meredith silently thanked Elizabeth Taylor for her famous White Diamonds, the only fragrance she ever wore.

They exited the elevator and Max, the doorman, jumped to open the heavy outer glass doors of the building.

As they walked towards the circular drive, a black town car approached and stopped. Paul reached for the door handle and followed Meredith into the car. They sat close, not touching, in the large comfortable back seat.

"Much more luxurious than the last time we were in a back seat together," he said with a smile.

"How can you remember so many things that went on years ago and besides we were never in the back seat, we were always in the front seat. That must have been one of your other girlfriends," and they both laughed together. No instruction was given to the driver and none was required she gathered.

Because of his work with the government, Paul had needed to ensure Meredith was safe to date, safe to travel with, and safe to love, so he immediately ran a background check on her, which she passed with flying colors. His only surprise was learning her son Stephen had been part of his Washington team for almost ten years. Paul would never have put two and two together that his Agent Evans was her son.

Knowing Meredith had cleared his security checks, when she inquired into his week Paul skipped over the government details, but was comfortable answering the other questions Meredith asked about his multiple ventures. He made his business sound much like any other construction company, but there was nothing normal about it. He wasn't allowed to tell her the truth. Not yet, and maybe not ever.

Meredith hardly realized they had driven over the bridge. They were in the downtown area when his driver stopped in front of a small hotel in the Gaslamp area of San Diego. It looked very discrete. She started to wonder just what would be served at dinner tonight and *would she be dessert*, as her dear friend Fanny Brice would say.

"Where are we, Paul?" Meredith inquired, as they walked through the brass doors of the very elegant hotel. Paul ushered her into the foyer and taking her arm guided her into a small room just off the lobby.

"This is one of my favorite places to dine and is the best-kept secret in San Diego," he replied.

Meredith wanted to ask how he knew so much about her city as he resided in DC, but she knew he traveled a great deal, and from the way he knew his way around, had been to this hotel before.

When they entered the room she took a tighter grip on his arm. Stunned by the beauty of the surroundings, she asked him, "How did you ever find this place?"

"It's mine," he said casually. He waited to see her reaction. There was none. "It's my hotel. Well truthfully, it's one of my corporation's holdings but since I own the corporation, I own the hotel, and this dining room is reserved exclusively for me."

"You own this entire hotel?" Meredith said with

shock in her voice. "Just who are you Mr. Richardson and what other secrets do you have?"

"It's a long story, just an investment," he replied. "It's not very large and only has ten suites. I use it for corporate board meetings and a drop-in when I travel. It's better than the large chain hotels and my room is always ready. No reservations are ever needed."

Paul ushered her to what she realized was the only table in the small dining room and she saw it was set for two. He pulled the chair out for her and as she sat, Meredith tried to take in the opulent furnishings and art surrounding her. Elegant oriental rugs covered polished teakwood floors. Even in the dim light, the art looked very, very original. She realized she no longer knew this man and was stunned this beautiful room was for his use alone.

A waiter appeared carrying an ornate sterling silver champagne bucket and what looked like a very special bottle of Dom Perignon. He showed Paul the label for his approval. Once Paul nodded, the waiter opened the bottle and began pouring a flute of the vintage champagne for Meredith.

"No gin and tonic tonight," Paul announced. "This is a special evening for two old friends to celebrate their reunion. I hope you agree." She nodded yes.

"To us," he added, reaching for his glass.

Meredith lifted her glass, a bit overwhelmed and wondering even more about this stalwart man sitting across from her. Just who was he now and what had become of the captain of the football team?

Following their first sip of the smooth champagne, Meredith searched her thoughts for just how to begin their conversation, finally settling on, "Tell me about your sons, Paul. If I remember, they are slightly older than my Stephen and Jennifer."

"They are," Paul responded. "Thirteen months separate my boys, with David being the younger brother of Paul Junior or PJ as our family calls him. PJ is smart, bold, and brash. He was an excellent athlete although he favored baseball rather than football."

"Our family are big baseball fans and follow the San Diego Padres. And son number two?" Meredith prompted.

"Unlike PJ, David is quiet, reserved, and studious. He loves tennis, books, and numbers. They joined the business full-time once they had their degrees."

"And where are they now?" Meredith asked.

"David lives in DC and handles our East Coast and European dealings. PJ lives back in the Phoenix area and is in charge of the West Coast and Far East businesses. Both of them seem to have inherited a large portion of my drive and determination, but I also see their mother's kindness in them."

"Are they married? Do you have grandchildren?"

"They are—PJ to Alison and David to Susan. Neither couple have children. Where are your children now?"

"As you know, I have three—a son and two daughters. Stephen is the oldest and he works for the government. He and his wife, Loren, have thirteen-year-old twins and are currently living in England. Next is Jennifer. She lives the closest to me in Indian Wells and took over my retail stores when I retired. She is not married but shares her life with a wonderful man, Stanley Barrington. And our youngest, Claire, is a lawyer in New York City, now divorced with one daughter."

Knowing how much she wished at least one of her children lived closer than three hours away, Meredith said, "It must be nice to have David and Susan living in the same city as you." Smiling, she continued, "It's too bad you don't have grandchildren. They are such fun to spoil and then send home to their parents."

As Meredith continued telling Paul about Claire and Heather Ann, a beautifully prepared dinner was served as if they were dining in the finest of restaurants. Small courses, each more delicious than the last. The main entree of veal with the most mouth-watering sauce was served by the chef himself and was the best Meredith had ever tasted.

"I see you keep a mystery chef hidden in the kitchen," she said.

Paul smiled and was quick to tell her he had a wonderful staff and a head chef he had hired away from one of his favorite New York City eateries. Meredith hesitated as the waiter began refilling her champagne, but it was so delicious she allowed him to fill her glass a second time.

Quiet music played and Paul reached across the table to take Meredith's hand. "I think this is our dance," he said and led her to the marble fireplace where a glowing fire burned. There was no dance floor, but the hearth was large enough for two.

"I think you have done this before, Mr. Richardson," she teased.

"Believe me, I haven't," Paul replied. "Dancing

isn't my strong suit, but it is a way to hold you in my arms."

Being back in a man's arms seemed almost strange to Meredith. Alex had been gone for three years and there had been no dancing as of late. It was the most romantic night she could remember in a very long while and she hoped she didn't seem an easy target for this generous man's affection.

As he drew her closer, her fears vanished and she didn't want to think. It was time to feel.

"Relax," Paul whispered. "We're just two old friends getting to know each other again. I will start slow, but promise I won't give up this time."

She turned her head to look up into his powerful face.

"I want you with me, Meredith, just as I did so long ago. We aren't kids in the front seat of a car anymore. We have experienced deep love and loss. I don't want to move too fast, but I have no one to share my life with. I know it's just been a short time since our surprising encounter in DC but this feels so right. We are together again, and we can offer each other so much."

Meredith closed her eyes and wanted to cry at his words. She pressed her face into his broad chest, and for the first time in a long time was at a loss for words. "This is all coming so fast," she managed to say. "It feels like a movie, and I am a bit too old to be in the starring role."

Paul lifted her face and softly kissed her on the lips. "You have always been my inspiration, you just didn't know it. I made love to my wife and saw you until the images grew dim, and now you are here in my arms and I am holding you again. Let's give ourselves a chance."

Meredith looked into his eyes and asked with a smile, "Could we just become friends again first?"

He pulled her close and surrounded her with his strong arms. "I would love to be your friend, Mrs. Evans," he said. They stood for a moment holding each other, not saying a word. The music had stopped, but neither noticed. The room was so quiet Meredith could hear his heartbeat. She couldn't believe what he had said. Loving words from a man was a gift, one she thought she would never receive again.

When the music resumed Meredith commented she had not danced in a very long time. "Well, I'm no Arthur Murray," Paul replied, and they both laughed as he attempted to twirl her. "I could hold you like this all night," he whispered, and she felt a thrill that had long since vanished. Neither spoke. It was as if they were both caught in the quiet satisfaction of being back in each other's arms.

Paul's plan was going well. He wasn't rushing her, but his tactics were working. She was quite impressed, but was she interested in a second chance at love?

Testing the waters as they started back to their lone table, Paul cautiously asked Meredith, "Would you like to have dessert and coffee upstairs in my suite?"

"Maybe next time," she responded. Pleased to hear there would be a next time, Paul waved the server over.

"Coffee, Madam?" asked the white-gloved waiter.

117

"Decaf, please," as her eyes sparkled at the sight of the decadent orange soufflé that had been placed in front of her. Meredith glanced over to see Paul checking his watch and suddenly realized it was almost eleven P.M. "You must be exhausted after your long flight from London."

Even though he would not admit it, he was tired. The week had been full of meetings and too many long flights to remote places.

After a few bites of her delicious soufflé, Meredith said, "I think we should be going." Paul nodded in agreement and rose first. He reached for her coat and placed it on her shoulders as she took one last look at the beautiful dining room, still surprised by who its owner was.

They left the elegant hotel and found the downtown streets deserted, but there at the curb was the black town car waiting for them with the same attendant holding the door. Once seated, Paul did not move toward Meredith as they rode back to the beach. They were both quiet. Meredith glanced towards Paul and could see his eyes heavy with sleep.

She thought of how much she had missed being in the company of a man. Paul gave her contentment and peace she had long since forgotten. The few casual dates she'd had since being widowed were certainly not like this. She wondered what would happen when they arrived at her apartment.

Paul's eyes may have been closed, but his mind was racing. He wanted her right now in the back seat of the car like a lovesick teenager, but he kept himself in check. He found his arm moving toward her shoulder, and as he rested it near her hair, she bent into the curve of his arm as if she belonged there. In his mind, she did.

Meredith was having her own thoughts. Would he try to kiss her goodnight? Maybe he wouldn't like the way she kissed. She hadn't been kissed in a very long time, maybe even forgotten how.

All too quickly, they were pulling into the roundabout in front of the El Cortez Building. The driver was quick to come around and open the door. Paul got out first and reached for Meredith's hand. This time she accepted it, and he held it for a long moment.

When she looked up, she saw the night doorman holding the large glass door open with a look of surprise on his face. He had never seen Mrs. Evans on the arm of anyone other than Mr. Evans. Good for her, he thought. She is an attractive lady who doesn't deserve to be alone. He activated the elevator and wished them a good evening, not knowing whether the gentleman would be leaving or staying the night.

As they exited the elevator and walked down the hall to her corner apartment, Meredith reached into her purse for her key. Paul extended his hand.

"Let me do the honors." Taking the key, he inserted it into the lock and held the door open for her as Alex had always done.

Once inside, Paul turned Meredith towards him. "I have been a gentleman all evening, but my patience is at its end and I really want to kiss you. Chastise me if you must—" and that was all he said before her arms went to his shoulders, and she pulled him towards her.

"I think we're both a bit impatient," she said as their lips met.

His kiss was soft at first and then searching as if he had been looking for her a very long time. She reacted in a way that shocked her as she clung to him and couldn't let go.

When they paused for breath, Meredith, her face in his chest said, "You must think me a sex-starved widow."

"Is that what you are?"

"No." She turned away. "I'm sorry, this is not like me to throw myself into a man's arms, but it has been such a beautiful night, sharing a romantic dinner with an old friend. I guess it was my way of saying thank you for the wonderful evening."

"Want to thank me again?" Paul joked, and caught her in his arms as she started to twist away. This time the kiss was hard, and when his lips left her mouth, they trailed down her neck. The boy she had known had become a man and he heard her suck in a breath that made his body quiver.

"Paul, this is getting out of hand for a first date."

"Meredith, we had our first date more than forty years ago after a football game, don't you remember? We have a lot to catch up on."

"I think we need some coffee," Meredith said, as she wiggled out of his arms. "It will have to be decaf, as we don't need any more stimulation tonight. I am going to have a difficult enough time sleeping. I will just be a few minutes."

Meredith rounded the kitchen door and had to steady herself against the wall. What was she doing in the arms of a man and responding like a schoolgirl to the football hero? Compose yourself Meredith, and get a grip as your grandchildren would say.

After making the coffee and setting two filled mugs on a small tray with cream and sugar, she reentered the living room, and saw he had taken her advice, kicked off his snakeskin loafers, and was stretched out on the couch fast asleep. She smiled and walked toward him. When he didn't stir, she took the tray back to the kitchen.

As she approached again, he awoke. Knowing he could not spend the night on the couch, Meredith knew it was time to offer him the guest room, in friendship, of course.

When he realized she was standing near, he said drowsily "If I lived here, I'd be home."

"Paul Richardson, how dare you make such a suggestion on our first date!"

She didn't budge from where she stood and said in a firm voice, "I have a guest room, and you're welcome to stay the night. I know you own a hotel, but it's so late, and we both need to be sensible."

Paul smiled and rolled his eyes. "Well, it's been years; what's one more night without you?" He reached for his shoes and realized he had definitely made himself at home. "Let me call Jake to have him take the car back." He reached for his cell phone and dialed as Meredith went to ready her guest room.

The room was done in tones of rust, gold, and brown, perfect for her male visitor. She laid out towels and even put a toothbrush and toothpaste on the counter. She was used to company and always had extra items her guests might have forgotten.

She opened the bathroom drawers and reached for the electric razor that had belonged to Alex. She kept it for Stephen in case he needed one. Could she offer this personal item to Paul? She decided it would be a nice gesture so she placed the razor on the counter, closed the drawer, and walked to the edge of the bed.

For years she had always turned down the bed for Alex. She hesitated, then walked to the head of the bed and was beginning to remove the throw pillows when she heard Paul say, "Do you leave a chocolate kiss too?"

He seemed to fill the door space with his size, and then he walked into the room.

"It's too late for chocolate," she said smiling. "Make yourself comfortable. Towels are on the bathroom counter and the room is yours."

"And yours," he added.

"Mine is down the hall, and that's where I'll stay."

Paul was too tired to argue and knew she was right. She didn't move toward him, but walked to the door, adding "sleep well," and quietly left the room, pulling the door closed behind her.

Taking a quick inventory of the toiletries she had set out for him, the sight of the toothbrush made him smile. He undressed, used the toothbrush, and sat down on the edge of her guest bed. Soon she would be in it with him if he had his way.

As he lay down, he again remembered that night on the river's edge and thought of his feelings at seeing her car drive away. He knew they had done the right thing but was surprised at how much doing the right thing had hurt. Now Rachel was gone, as was

Alex Evans, and tomorrow was a new beginning in this chapter of their lives. Paul laid his head on the pillow, closed his eyes, and was asleep within a few minutes.

Meredith walked into her bedroom and looked at the bed. She had to close her eyes to avoid what she was thinking—Paul lying there with arms outstretched, beckoning her to join him. Was she out of her mind?

She went into the bathroom to escape the view and undressed. She chose a nightgown that would cover her gracefully and laid the matching robe at the foot of the bed. She slid between the cool sheets and turned off the light, suddenly missing the sensual warmth of a man. It had been quite an evening, and she looked forward to learning more about the handsome man in the next room.

Paul wasn't asleep for long when he woke abruptly. On an impulse, he walked across the hall to Meredith's door but stopped before knocking. Determined to make their re-acquaintance last, Paul knew moving too fast might scare her away again, so he turned, went back to his bed, and waited for sleep to find him once again.

Lurking in the shadows of the parking circle, neither Meredith nor Paul noticed the large man's silhouette or the glow of his cigarette as he stared up at her patio door. He saw her though and knew she was not alone. But he was patient and could wait.

Meredith woke to the sound of a cell phone ringing. The sun was barely up and she heard soft, muffled tones coming from the guest room. Within a few minutes, she heard the shower turn on and a short time later the sound of a razor. Paul was shaving and using Alex's razor.

She put on her robe, brushed through her hair, dabbed on a bit of lipstick, and walked toward the aroma of fresh brewing coffee coming from the kitchen where she had pre-programmed the coffee maker to start early for Paul. He stood writing something on a pad, and she suddenly realized he was leaving.

"Good morning, Sunshine," Paul said, as he came toward her and placed a kiss on the top of her head. "I have an emergency at one of my construction sites and will be gone until at least the weekend, maybe even longer. Then it's off to solve a problem in the Pacific. Will you join me?" he asked. "I can give you a firm date later in the week."

"Where to?" Meredith questioned.

"Honolulu, for about five days. Meetings for my Navy projects should take a couple of days to wrap up and I can throw a few extra fun days in the sun for both of us. Want to be daring and just pick up and go?"

"I—I don't know, Paul," she stumbled.

"You have a few days to get ready and you don't need to take much. We can buy anything you need when we get there." He looked deep into her eyes and added, "Meredith, don't think, just do," and with a quick kiss he turned and was out the door.

Drop everything? But could she? What about the

children, appointments, and did he say leave in a few days? Could she be that daring? After two cups of very strong coffee, her decision was made and she called Paul's Mrs. Parker to confirm she was indeed available for the trip.

By the afternoon she was anxious to talk to someone about her upcoming adventure. But who? She wasn't ready to tell her children; they might not approve. Dr. Karen, if she could reach her, would be the perfect person. She placed the call to DC on Karen's private number and was pleased to hear her friend's voice on the line after the second ring.

"Karen, I have exciting news for you." She told her all about the romantic dinner at the exclusive hotel he admitted to owning and ended with Paul's invitation to go to Honolulu. "He wants me to go with him."

Jokingly, Meredith asked Karen to go along. "I think we may need a chaperone."

Karen did not seem surprised about any of Meredith's revelations. "Men like Paul have investments all over the world. And at your age, what you each need is some great no-nonsense sex," and they both laughed again.

"Oh Karen, I couldn't!"

"Last I heard, sex didn't have any age limit and I have taught many a sex class."

Meredith questioned her about what to tell the children. Maybe nothing, they both agreed. "Just say you are going away with an old friend and forget to mention the sex of the friend." They laughed again, then sent their love to each other and signed off.

Meredith fussed with house details, but the small

125

condo didn't take much effort to care for and after finishing another cup of coffee and her favorite banana bread took off for her morning walk down the boardwalk to the historic Hotel del Coronado.

Mrs. Parker called Meredith a few days later and confirmed Paul would be arriving Sunday to pick her up for their trip.

The next few days were spent arranging for mail pickup and talking with Max, the doorman, letting him know she would be gone for possibly a week. Stephen and Loren, and Claire, were too far away to even miss her. She did, however, need to tell Jennifer. She called the store on purpose, hoping Jen would be too busy to ask many questions. As usual, Jennifer was in a hurry and told her to have a good time and not talk to strangers, never thinking the friend her mom was traveling with might be a man.

As Meredith replaced the receiver, she wondered how many times her children had lied to her just to save her feelings. She wasn't lying, she just hadn't told the entire truth. Well, it's my turn, she thought, and it isn't a real lie. I am just avoiding some of the details.

With that thought in mind, she smiled to herself and reached into the closet for her favorite rolling luggage. She felt like a schoolgirl taking her first adventure. After all, wasn't that what she was doing?

She packed carefully. Her new beach cover-up and best swimsuit were first in the suitcase. Next came two pairs of her favorite white pants, an oversized shirt, and a few tops. Her makeup bag was always ready, and Paul had told her to travel light.

The nightwear could be a problem. Something not too thin and with a matching robe would definitely be in order.

What was she doing? Choosing nightwear in case he might see her in it? He would offer her a separate bedroom, wouldn't he? Confused about what to expect, she put her nightgown and robe in the case and closed the lid.

It was a five-and-a-half-hour flight from San Diego to Honolulu and she thought food would be served. Just in case, she tucked her usual desperation snack, a package of peanut butter crackers, into her travel tote bag. She knew first class was expensive and hoped with all his business miles he would upgrade them, at least to business class.

Was she in for the surprise of her life?

CHAPTER 10

Meredith barely slept Saturday night. When her phone rang Sunday at 7:30 a.m., she woke with a start to hear Paul saying, "Good morning, Sunshine." That now seemed to be his favorite name for her. "Sorry if I woke you but I have been locked in government meetings for the past few days. Are you packed and ready?"

"Yes," she replied in an excited voice.

He told her he would be there in a couple of hours to pick her up. Over the past days, Paul had thought often of Meredith and their impending travel. He reminded himself he wasn't going to push her this time. She would have to make up her mind and want to be in his life again.

Meredith did a last-minute check of her suitcase, hair, and makeup just as the doorbell rang. She had called the doorman to allow Paul upstairs and was surprised when she opened the door to find Paul's driver instead.

Before she could ask, he announced "Good morning, Mrs. Evans. I'm Mr. Paul's driver, Jake. He is tied up in a meeting and will meet us at the plane."

Though she was disappointed Paul was not there to pick her up, Meredith politely responded, "It's nice to meet you, Jake. If you'll take my bags, I will lock the door and be right with you."

Jake directed her to the waiting town car and Meredith settled herself in the back seat. He was a quiet man, but under his black suit she suspected lurked a large body frame. For one nervous moment, she surmised he might be a bodyguard. Was the construction business dangerous enough for Paul to need a bodyguard? Well, maybe some of the international projects, she thought.

After a few miles of silence, she mustered up enough courage to ask Jake how long he had worked for Paul. "I've been with Mr. Paul for many years," he replied, and she suspected that was all he would say. They must have a deep past for Jake to be so loyal, she thought. When she knew Paul better, she would ask him about his relationship with this mysterious man. For now, she and Jake rode the rest of the way in silence.

The San Diego airport was familiar to Meredith as over the years she was often traveling herself or picking up a guest or two. The children had told her to stay busy and travel, but somehow, she felt this wasn't the type of trip they had in mind for her.

The route Jake took bypassed the main terminal, which made Meredith a bit nervous. When they turned into the gate marked Executive Aircraft she inquired where they were going. He replied, "To meet Mr. Paul."

As they drove down the tarmac Jake was talking to someone on one of his multiple cell phones. Meredith assumed it was Paul.

When the car slowed, Meredith was staring at

three letters on the tail of a very large airplane. RCC. She couldn't believe her eyes. It was as large as most commercial airliners. Did Richardson Construction Company own a private jet of this size?

The car stopped at the foot of the stairs and Jake rushed around to open the door for her. As she stepped out, her eyes traveled up the stairs. Standing at the top, smiling down at her was Paul. Meredith shook her head in disbelief. There he was, looking handsome and relaxed in slacks and a Polo shirt. She tried not to look surprised as he walked down to meet her. As he neared her, a warm smile broke across his face.

"I didn't want to frighten you with all my toys," he said.

"Oh yes, some toy," she said with a smile in her voice.

He took her arm and led her up the stairs. Nothing could have prepared her for what she was about to see.

"Paul, this is unbelievable, and here I felt sorry for you, up all night on the red-eye from London."

He smiled. "It's not so tough when you travel this way," he admitted.

They entered into a living room. No ordinary row seats for this aircraft. It was furnished with a small couch flanked by two side chairs. The floors were carpeted in a deep beige tone with colorful oriental rugs strewn in strategic walking areas. There was a game table next to the window, a large television, and phones discreetly placed about the room.

"Come, I will show you your room."

"My room?" she exclaimed.

Paul smiled and added, "You may want to rest."

Just what was on his mind she wondered and why would she need to rest?

They entered the small bedroom cabin and her suitcase had already been laid on the bed. She sat her purse on the dresser and suddenly felt very shy. She laughed at the thought of the peanut butter crackers stowed away in her handbag and reached to hand them to Paul. "I guess we don't need these, do we?"

Paul smiled, laughed, held her hand to his lips, and kissed it. "Let's have a toast to a wonderful few days." He took the hand he had just kissed and led her back to the living room. "Thirsty?" he asked. "The bar is always open."

"How soon do we leave?" she questioned.

"Whenever you're ready. How about a glass of champagne first?"

"Sounds perfect." Within seconds, as if he had pushed a button, the champagne arrived on a silver tray carried by a uniformed male attendant.

Paul raised his glass toward her in a toast. "To our finding each other after all these years."

As they touched glasses, it was as if their souls touched. They gazed into each other's eyes, and Meredith couldn't resist the sudden urge to touch his face. Her hand went to his cheek, and the look in his eyes said thank you.

"If you pinch me, will I wake up on Southwest?"

Paul laughed and pinched her on the arm. "See, no Southwest."

The pilot announced they were next in line for

takeoff.

"We need to move to our seats and buckle up. Let me take your glass." Again, their hands touched, and Meredith felt a warm glow and a slow fire building. Was it the champagne, the private jet, Paul, or all three?

The roar of the engine signaled their takeoff, but Meredith felt she was already soaring. The plane climbed over the blue Pacific as smooth as glass. After a few moments, the pilot announced the seat belt sign was turned off and at that moment one of the phones began to ring.

"Excuse me," Paul said, taking the call with a series of yeses and no comments.

"I requested a few days of vacation, but I guess the government brass didn't get the memo."

Meredith was just going to question what the brass wanted when a beautiful tray of hors d'oeuvres was presented.

"I suppose Jake whipped them up in his kitchen."

"No, not exactly, but you must like to cook, and I am trying to impress you."

"How do you know I like to cook?" she replied.

"You are just too gracious not to have mastered the kitchen."

"I love to give parties and I do know how to drive to Costco."

He laughed as he took her hand. "Come, I'll give you the tour. By the way," he added with a smile, "I have stock in Costco." And somehow, she was sure he did.

The kitchen, which he called the galley, had the look of a well-equipped restaurant. It was sleek, stainless, and ready to prepare a gourmet meal. Standing in his white jacket was the chef from Paul's hotel restaurant in San Diego.

"The boss has perks, doesn't he?" Meredith said.

They wandered through to the small dining room where the table was beautifully set for two, which by now was no surprise. Baccarat crystal, elegant china, and sterling silver graced the table with exotic Hawaiian flowers as a centerpiece.

"If this is set for lunch, what do we do for dinner?" she joked.

"Whatever you desire," Paul replied, and she had a feeling she knew just what he meant. He again took her hand and walked her to the cockpit door.

"Have you ever flown a plane before?"

"No, and I'm not starting now." He knocked on the door and Meredith was shocked to see Jake at the controls.

"Do you drive everything for Mr. Paul?"

"Almost," he replied.

"Jake doesn't say much," she said, as they continued with their tour. "So, this is how you live, flying from place to place and office to office."

He led her through the living room into the master suite. He stepped back at the door of his bedroom. The room was decorated in almost the same tones as Meredith's guest room in Coronado.

"See why I felt so at home in your house," he said. "By the way thanks for the toothbrush. It was a great touch. Do you leave one out for all your men friends?"

"Only my special ones." They laughed together.

Paul turned her to him there in his bedroom and

held her in his arms.

"Something has brought us together. I was afraid to overwhelm you with my lifestyle, but it's who I am. I live everywhere and nowhere. If we capture the moment, we can make each other very happy. I have been hoping for someone to share my life with, and now by accident, I run into you, the first woman I ever loved. A chance dinner party in DC brought you back in my life."

Just like in the movies, the plane hit a bit of turbulence and Meredith fell against Paul.

His arms were around her in an instant, and before either knew what was happening, his lips closed on hers. Meredith's arms went around his back. She had to hold on to him to keep her balance.

They were both breathless and trembling and standing beside his bed. They weren't kids and knew what came next. His arms moved down her back and pulled her close.

Her mind was racing. Two naked over sixty bodies scared her to death. She had taken care of herself all of her life, but it was for Alex who accepted her aging body. Would this exciting executive who owned hotels, private jets, and could have any woman he wanted, expect more than she had to offer?

Meredith had never made love to any man but Alex, yet here she stood in the arms of a new man, overwhelmed with desire.

"Stop, please," she gasped and inhaled a gulp of air. "I would like to know more about you than a dinner, lunch, and a night in my guest room."

He released her with a reluctant smile and

admitted he was moving too fast. "Guess I just want to make up for all the years we've lost."

"Can you wait until after lunch?" she joked.

"Is that a promise?"

"No, it's an *I'll-think-about-it promise*."

"Well then, let's have lunch so you can start to think about it." He took her hand and reluctantly led her back into the dining room.

Lunch was perfectly served by the chef and a uniformed waiter. Paul and Meredith talked about their lives, children, business, and their loneliness. Meredith needed to be honest with Paul, and as she walked him through her life, it made him realize how happy she had been. They talked of her grandchildren and she admitted unbearable loneliness after Alex died.

When she finished, Paul smiled at her softly and then continued with the story he had begun at their luncheon in DC.

"I have never told another soul, and maybe it's the wine. The wild romps with secretaries are long gone." Sex in the nineties became dangerous, and he shyly admitted to watching a few X-rated videos in hotel rooms to get him through the lonely nights. "I have not been to bed with a woman in a while, maybe even forgot how," he joked. "When I saw you at that dinner party I couldn't believe my eyes. I know we're older, but I want you, and I desperately hope you want me, too."

Tears filled her eyes as she remembered her feelings on that dusty riverbank so long ago. "It took all my strength to get in the car and drive away from you so many years ago. After Alex was taken from me, I never thought romance would come into my life again, and here you are.

"Lunch is finished. Are you ready for dessert?" she said with a devilish smile. Paul took her extended hand and guided her to his bedroom.

He knew they were due to land in Honolulu in a short while. "Shall I tell Jake to put us in a holding pattern?" She nudged his leg and smiled. He pressed a button and a do-not-call light appeared.

Meredith took off her jacket and laid it on the leather chair beside the bed. "I am not twenty-five anymore."

"I sit behind a desk all day, eat late, and haven't exercised in a long time. Too busy to go to the gym," he joked, "and my experience these last years in the sex department is very limited." They both laughed, and the laughter helped to ease the tension between them.

Paul was quick to add, "It's been so long, it may be over quick, but it won't be the next time."

He reached to unbutton the front of her silk blouse and pushed it off her shoulders along with her bra straps. As his hands touched her, she felt a wave of excitement mixed with apprehension.

He was holding her breasts once again, as he had held them on the river's edge, but they were now his and he could finally possess her body as he had always dreamed.

"Maybe we should wait till dark," she said with a smile.

"Oh, let's be daring." But he lowered the window shades near the side of the bed. "There, feel more

137

comfortable?" Paul was pleased to hear her say *yes* as he guided her onto the bed and leaned to kiss her.

As his arms encircled her she knew this was right. They needed each other, and the time was now. She held his head in her hands while he kissed one breast and then the other. They were no longer firm, but he didn't seem to mind.

She played with the buttons on his shirt, and he brought his hands up to help her. In a few minutes, he was stripped of the shirt and instantly immersed in her warm body. He kissed her deeply and her arms encircled him.

She pulled him closer and found herself the aggressor. Meredith needed him and knew how much he wanted her. Sexual feelings had been a big part of her married life. Needs long-suppressed re-emerged. Meredith could feel his large erection against her leg, and the excitement was overwhelming. Suddenly she was no longer the shy young girl in the front seat of the football jock's car. As they quickly shed the rest of their clothes, all she wanted was to have his hands on her body.

Paul could not control himself and whispered, "I need you now, please. Next time I'll take longer, but I need you now."

As if waiting for an invitation, when he heard her whisper *yes,* he rolled on top of her and silently entered the place he had dreamed of being most of his life. He was home at last.

Meredith held him tightly as he climaxed. Paul kissed her gently then rolled over and lay beside her.

"Not too shabby for the over sixty crowd," he commented, and they both laughed. "Can we continue this on the ground? I think we are landing unless you want me to have Jake put us in that holding pattern I mentioned."

Meredith smiled and said, "Let's not traumatize Jake and the rest of the crew too much."

As Paul raised the shade of the airplane window, Meredith looked at the magical sight with all the hotels gleaming at the ocean's edge.

"What a beautiful city," she commented.

"I am more intrigued by the beautiful sight of the woman standing before me."

"Oh yes, I bet I am a sight. My hair is a mess, my makeup is off, as are my clothes. Are you blind?"

"Yes," he replied, "blind in love with you."

"That's not love, that's lust—the other 'L' word," Meredith said. "We just found each other and I can't believe we had sex on the second date." She crawled back in bed half-dressed, grabbed the pillow, and covered her face laughing.

"Meredith, our first date was over forty years ago, remember?"

Just then a quiet reminder came over the speaker located above the do-not-call button. They would be landing in fifteen minutes. Meredith smiled as she realized the truth behind the United Airline commercial. She had just flown *The Friendly Skies* and it was exciting and wonderful.

They pulled themselves together, and as they stood in the doorway leaving the bedroom Meredith blushed slightly as she asked, "Do you think Jake will know what we have been doing?"

"Not to worry. If he does, he is too polite to say a word," Paul responded with a soft smile.

He planted a kiss on the top of her head, adding, "Airplane sex is exciting. I can't wait for the return flight and just think what might happen in-between."

Slipping under his arm, she took her seat. Paul reached to strap her in for the landing. As the latch clicked, he whispered, "Here's to our Friendly Skies."

The descent and landing were as smooth as the sex they had both just experienced. Meredith's mind was still in the sky, and she could hardly believe what she had done with a man she had only found again a few short weeks ago.

What would her children think of their mother having sex on an airplane? She only hoped they would someday have the chance to find out.

CHAPTER 11

They disembarked the plane in Honolulu at the private executive terminal. There at the foot of the stairs stood the always-ready black town car.

Meredith had not been to Hawaii since the eighties, but the sights and sounds of the city of Honolulu seemed familiar. She could not have been happier when they turned up the long circular driveway of her favorite hotel on the island, The Hilton Hawaiian Village. She smiled to herself remembering the times she and Alex had been driven up this same driveway.

They were greeted at the entrance to the hotel by a bevy of bellmen. A beautiful large Oriental rug still covered the great stone entry and the view of the Koi Pond and the Pacific Ocean beyond took her breath away. The surroundings were well-known to her and Paul also seemed to know his way around. Had he brought other women here?

As they walked through the open-air lobby, her eyes traveled to the eighteenth floor of the Rainbow Tower. She blushed with the memory of what happened on the balcony of room 1813.

Check-in was not needed, and they were ushered to a private elevator marked Ali'I Tower. When the elevator doors opened on the penthouse floor, they were standing in a foyer, and in front of them was a large round marble table graced with breathtaking tropical flowers.

The suite was beautifully appointed and Paul took her hand as they walked to the balcony railing that surrounded the living room. He put his arms around her. She didn't move.

"This is too perfect," he heard her say, and took that as his cue to ask her about the sleeping arrangements.

"This is a two-bedroom suite. Do you want your own bedroom?"

"Will you think more of me if I said I would like my own room?"

He turned her to face him. "I have thought of you over the years and sometimes even imagined you in my arms. I want you with me in my bed, but it has to be your decision."

She looked into his eyes and was surprised by her quick response. "Yes, I want to be with you, too. Will you show me to our room?"

Paul pulled her to him, and they stood holding each other, words not necessary.

Meredith suggested a moonlight walk after they unpacked and were settled. Paul smiled in response. As they walked toward the bedroom, he asked her about dinner. Meredith realized the early evening hour and told him a snack would be fine for her, depending on how hungry he was.

"I am only hungry for you," he replied. Meredith smiled.

Looking around the bedroom she would soon be sharing with Paul, she calculated the size of the hotel suite and realized it was larger than her entire condo in Coronado. The bathroom was fantastic with a large oval tub big enough for three, beautiful marble sinks, gold faucets, and wonderful fluffy white towels. Soft lighting graced the room and seemed to transform her.

"A woman could get used to this," she said out loud.

Meredith heard Paul on the phone, and knowing his busy life, sensed he must have business going on around the world at all times of the day and night. She did not take the liberty of unpacking his suitcase, and after hanging up her few outfits, wondered if she brought the right clothes for these beautiful surroundings.

She dressed in a simple coral silk caftan with slits up the sides and her favorite gold sandals. She did a quick touch-up of her makeup, brushed her teeth, and was ready for their moonlight walk.

Paul hung up the phone as she approached and leaned back against the couch.

"You look lovely. Give me just a minute to change and we will go for our walk." He came back wearing a floral Hawaiian shirt, walking shorts, and loafers. "Ready?" He extended his hand and she took it without reservations.

As they walked down the beach hand in hand, he smiled and said, "I feel like a kid again strolling with my best girl."

"Let's not rush things," she replied.

"At my age, I don't want to go slow," Paul said.

The hotel had added new benches along the wide sidewalk that directs you through the Army Museum

Park near the Sheraton Waikiki. Was she mistaken or had a few new palm trees also been added to the landscape?

They sat staring at the waves. "How could you read my mind?" Meredith asked. "This is one of my favorite places in the entire world. I have even sat on this very beach a few times."

Paul took her hand and asked, "Does it bring back good memories?"

"Yes, I'm thinking of how happy we were here many years ago, but I am starting a new chapter of my life, one I thought I would never write. Alex would want me to be happy. I know he is looking down on me, smiling and a bit jealous I ran into you."

They stood and walked hand in hand back towards the hotel. As they rounded the bend, Meredith saw a blanket spread out, complete with an ice bucket, two back pillows, and a couple of beach towels. Sitting near the blanket on a rock was Jake holding what looked like a fancy carryout box. Jake sure stays busy, she thought.

"Thought you two might like a bit of dinner. I took the liberty of opening the wine and added a few snacks. I have been sampling them waiting for you."

"You read my mind, Jake, and many thanks. Dinner on the beach is just what the doctor ordered."

As Jake walked away, Paul took Meredith's hand and helped her down to the blanket. "You may have to help me up when it's time to leave," she said.

Paul joined her on the blanket and leaned over, taking her hands in his. "I hope I can help you with more than that." He kissed her deeply and her arms reached around him.

"Brazen, aren't we?" she managed to say before his lips claimed hers again. Her mouth opened and his tongue sought hers hungrily. Her dress had no access he noticed but he could feel her breasts coming alive under the soft silk and the kiss lingered for what seemed like forever. The bulge in his walking shorts could not go unnoticed.

"Would you think me a wanton woman if I asked you to make love to me here on the beach?"

He kissed her with so much passion she realized she had his answer. She struggled to unbutton his walking shorts while Paul wrestled with her caftan. "How can I get into this thing?" he asked in a frustrated voice.

"It does come up," and she reached to help him raise the long dress to her hips. For once she was glad she had listened to her friend Meg and switched to sexier underwear, but it would not have mattered to Paul.

Jake had conveniently left a lightweight throw over the picnic basket and it made a perfect cover-up for both of them. "Remind me to give him a raise," Paul said with a smile in his voice.

He entered her knowing at that moment only sexual contact could bring them both satisfaction. Nothing mattered as they moved together, gently at first, and then suddenly so hard it shook them both. He buried his face in her neck as he climaxed. Meredith clung to him as he whispered, "Love me."

When their hearts stopped racing, they began to calm down and gain control of their senses. After straightening their clothes, Meredith tossed off the light throw and said, "We just had sex under the stars, and we didn't even get arrested. How about a glass of wine to celebrate?"

As Paul poured the wine, he informed her, "Not to worry. I know the Honolulu police chief and have a lifelong get-out-of-jail-free card." And she was quite sure he did.

Meredith dipped into the basket to see what treasures Jake had supplied. She found two sandwiches that looked mouthwatering and some cookies. She set up their picnic dinner and Paul raised his glass in a toast. "To us, and to love at any age."

They ate their small meal and talked of the beauty of the hotel and its surroundings. Afterward, she moved to nestle in his arms and sat between his legs. He groaned when her body rubbed up against him. With his arms around her, Paul said, "Unless you want to make love again right here, we better go upstairs."

"Race you," she laughed.

"Nothing like two anxious seniors eager for sex," he said with a laughing voice.

He reached down to help Meredith up and they walked hand in hand back to the hotel.

They left the basket and blanket where it was, as Paul knew Jake would be along to take care of the remnants of their picnic. When they reached the elevator, they were still laughing but a bit breathless.

"We forgot it's uphill on the way back," Paul said, panting slightly.

Once the elevator door closed, they were again in each other's arms. She couldn't get enough of him and was shocked by her sexual appetite.

The door opened into their private lobby and they

moved toward the bedroom never leaving each other's side. When they got to the door Meredith found the bed turned down and orchids on the pillows. The room smelled so sweet and looked like a lover's hideaway.

"I need a minute to get undressed," she told Paul. She noticed someone had unpacked his suitcase, and his clothes were hung beside hers in the spacious closet. They looked like they belonged together.

Paul was in the living room closing down the suite as she sat at the dressing table staring at the woman in the mirror. Was that woman really her?

Meredith didn't hear him approach on the quiet carpet and suddenly realized he was standing behind her. He leaned down to kiss her neck.

"I could get used to this," he said.

"Paul, today was wonderful." He wanted to make love to her again but also needed her to be comfortable with the sleeping arrangements. He felt it might be awkward for Meredith to sleep with a man in her bed after all this time. He suggested they retire and just lie together, relax and get used to one another.

Meredith felt strange being in bed with another man. Her mind flashed to Alex. They seemed so much alike, Paul and Alex. Was Paul becoming an extension of Alex? He turned out the light but didn't reach for her.

"Shall we continue this tomorrow?" he said as he placed a kiss on her shoulder, and in the darkness, he heard her utter *thank you for understanding*.

Within two minutes she heard his soft breathing and knew he was fast asleep. She rolled toward him and before she knew it was also drifting off, feeling content for the first time in a very long while.

CHAPTER 12

Meredith woke to an aroma she recognized, her favorite Hawaiian Kona coffee. Paul was still sleeping, so who made the coffee? Not wanting to wake him, she slipped out of bed without a sound. Putting on her robe she followed the coffee aroma to the balcony and of course, there stood Jake.

"Coffee, Ma'am? How does The Mrs. take her coffee?" Jake asked.

"Black with two sugars," she replied, and was quick to add, "Won't you call me Meredith?"

"Yes ma'am, Mrs. Meredith."

"How about just Meredith?"

"As you wish," he replied, but she somehow knew it would always be Mrs. Meredith. "You are very dedicated to Paul. How long have you two been friends?"

"Many years," was all he answered, and she knew that conversation was over.

She quickly changed the subject asking, "How does Mr. Paul take his coffee?"

"Black, and very strong. You are good for Mr. Paul. I wish you both well." Meredith was sure she blushed, as Jake had to know what was going on between them.

She reached for the two cups of coffee and

walked towards the bedroom and the man still asleep in the very large bed. She saw him roll over reaching for her and she smiled. He seemed startled she wasn't there and was quick to open his eyes. When he saw her standing over him with the two cups of coffee, he said sleepily, "I see Sunshine beat me up today."

"Yes, I did," The sight of the woman he loved bringing him coffee in bed made his heart soar.

"Thank you for last night and not rushing things. It was so comforting to have you next to me." He reached for her, but she put the coffee in his hand instead and sat down next to him on the bed.

"I won't rush you, Meredith, but I do want you in my life."

Meredith smiled and added a quick, "I want that too, but I think Jake is waiting to talk to you on the terrace. By the way, how did he get in to prepare the coffee?"

"Jake knows all. We have been through a lot together, and he is a very close and trusted friend."

"He has great respect for you and watches out for you. I feel you share the same regard for him. Is he your bodyguard?" Meredith asked.

"That's a story for another time," he responded. "What would you like to do on this beautiful Hawaiian day, besides bring me morning coffee?"

"A relaxing day on the beach would be wonderful."

"What, no day pampering yourself at the spa?"

"No, I leave that for my daughters. A day in the sun has always been my favorite thing to do until I ran into an old friend with a few better ideas."

"Okay, a day in the sun it shall be, but first I need

to talk to Jake and make a few phone calls." Meredith smiled, not at all surprised.

"I'll go change, and you can let me know when you're ready to go downstairs."

A while later they arrived down at the beach and found large padded lounge chairs stacked with white fluffy towels. The island temperature was perfect. They relaxed and talked of their families, of lifelong friends, businesses, and the future.

The hours flew by and the book Meredith had brought from DC remained closed. When she noticed Paul's eyes growing heavy she closed her eyes pretending to sleep and in a few minutes, he was asleep. Memories of Alex flooded her heart. She remembered him sleeping on the beach, one of the few places he would ever nap. Did she love them both? Looking over at the gentle man resting beside her, she knew she did.

How had her life taken such an unexpected and amazing turn in such a short time?

A late lunch of fresh fruit, cheeses, and mouthwatering small fish sandwiches was served on a wooden pallet delivered by the staff of the Village. They discovered individual macadamia nut chocolates nestled among the Hawaiian flowers.

Following lunch, they strolled through the variety of shops at the Rainbow Bazaar in the Village. As they entered Na Hoku, Paul noticed a brilliant necklace of three diamonds. Seeing his interest, the clerk removed it from the case and handed it to Paul.

"This is a lovely gift for your lady," the clerk commented.

Paul reached for the necklace and carefully clasped it around Meredith's slender neck.

"Oh Paul, it is exquisite," she said as she looked at her reflection in the mirror on the counter.

"And it fits you perfectly, my love," he said as he signed the tab.

Meredith had never received such an extravagant gift. Uninvited, doubts crept in and she wondered how many other women had received such a gift from Paul Richardson. Then she felt him kiss her neck and saw him smiling at her in the mirror, and as she leaned back into his chest, those thoughts went right out of her head.

Paul had two business meetings later in the day, and Meredith returned to the beach alone. After a while, she decided to try the spa Paul had suggested. She had never experienced such luxury and found she thoroughly enjoyed the massage and warm body wrap.

When the masseuse finished, Meredith barely made it upstairs to the suite where she crawled in bed and was asleep within minutes. Paul found her there and looking down at her, wished he could come home to her every night. He sat on the edge of the bed, and she stirred. "Wake up, Sunshine," he whispered.

"Oh Paul, it was a wonderful day," she purred, still trying to wake herself from the relaxing afternoon nap. "Did you have anything special planned for tonight?" she inquired.

"How does a romantic dinner with a handsome man sound?"

"And just whom might that be," she joked.

"Rise and shine, Sunshine, unless you want me to crawl in bed with you?"

She quietly sat up and replied, "I'm starved."

"I'm here," he said with a smile in his voice.

"No, for food," and they both laughed.

When she was more awake and had finished dressing, she walked out to the living room which had again been transformed into a private dining room for two. Candles were burning, music was playing and cocktails were ready.

"How do you do all this?" She was quick to ask as he walked over to meet her.

Paul took her in his arms, and his face came so close she thought she would die from wanting him to touch her.

Arms entwined, he kissed her and brushed his lips back and forth over hers until she opened her mouth to him. Meredith pressed herself even closer. His tongue found hers and they danced the most exciting dance she could remember.

"Do we have to have dinner now?" Paul whispered.

"No," Meredith replied, "I have suddenly lost my appetite, for food that is."

They turned to go back to the bedroom but never made it. Paul stopped at the large plush couch and began shedding his clothes. The simple shift she wore was suddenly on the floor and they lay together naked, each trying to entice the other. Paul took time to pleasure her in ways she had forgotten, arousing feelings in her so natural they surprised her. She rolled over to meet him, and as he entered her, she locked her legs around him as they moved in perfect harmony. This time they climaxed together, and it was minutes before either let go.

Meredith finally rose, picked up her caftan, and wrapped it around her waist as she went into the bedroom to put herself back together. She thought how much easier it was for the man. My makeup is a mess and this sure makes us late for dinner.

When she walked back into the living room Paul said with a quirky smile, "Now that you have had your way with me, what you would like for dinner?"

"We could send out for pizza," she joked.

Paul was quick to say, "I was raised on pizza. How did you know?"

"Order extra cheese and pepperoni for me and leave off the anchovies," she added, and he was quick to agree nothing was too good for his favorite girl. He reached for the phone but instead of dialing room service decided to surprise her.

She noticed the table had been reset with fresh ice in the glasses. "Looks like the gremlins have been here again. I guess someone knew we would be hungry." They walked to the terrace. Both seemed so relaxed words were not needed.

"How about a moonlight swim after our pizza?"

Paul, surprised at Meredith's invitation, said, "I thought you never got your hair wet."

"Oh, I never do."

He smiled, and said, "You may tonight," and she knew he was not talking about the hair on the top of her head.

The pizza arrived from a local restaurant, along with the most wonderful salad, individual small lasagnas, and a vintage bottle of Pinot Noir. It was a perfect way to end their even more perfect day.

After dinner, they changed and went to the private pool reserved for guests of the Ali'I Tower. It was deserted and the view over the pool to the ocean below was spectacular.

The water was warm, and they walked in holding hands. Paul swam a lap or two and then lounged on the pool steps. Meredith floated to him, and his long arms reached to embrace her. The water made them feel light, free, and so peaceful.

The large bulge in his swimsuit could not go unnoticed. As he pulled Meredith deep against his chest, she encircled his head with her arms.

"Meredith, I want you inside, outside, and poolside." He kissed her with such passion and her legs naturally floated around him in the warm water, holding her closer to him. He groaned when she rubbed against him. "I think it's time to go to our room," Paul was quick to say.

"Just a few minutes longer," she begged while trailing kisses down his neck. "Here would be more fun."

"Let's go upstairs instead," he said. and he gently broke free from her and caught hold of her hand to pull her out of the water. He reached for the towels lying on the lounge chair, covered Meredith's shoulders as he had done forty years ago, and wrapped one around his waist.

"My, my, you're anxious," she laughed.

When they entered their private elevator, he pulled her into his arms. "You make me feel like a love-crazed teenager."

"We are," she said. "We are just older and wiser

teenagers."

"Let's make love right here in the elevator," Paul suggested. "We can stop between floors."

"We could also get arrested," she laughed. "I heard they have cameras in these things."

"You're worth it."

"But think of my reputation," she said, sounding like a damsel in distress.

When the elevator door opened all too quickly to suit Paul, they tore apart long enough to walk towards the bedroom. As they passed through the living room where the candles were ablaze, music was playing, and lights were low, Meredith had another idea. "It's a glorious night, and it seems a shame to crush all those beautiful flowers covering the bed." She reached for his hand and led Paul to the terrace where she knew luxurious padded outdoor furniture awaited them.

"Let's call this our bedroom tonight," she said in her most seductive voice. "Do you think me presumptuous to suggest such ideas?"

Paul smiled at her and said, "I think the urge to pleasure and surprise each other is exciting. I feel I am just beginning to discover you."

He reclined on the chaise lounge and drew Meredith down on top of him, pulling her swimsuit down to her waist. Her full breasts fell free into his hands.

"Make love to me, Meredith," he whispered.

No longer shy, Meredith stood and removed her bathing suit while Paul struggled out of his. She sank down on his erection as she straddled him. They moved together in perfect rhythm as if they had been lovers for years. Their excitement peaked, and both climaxed at what seemed the same moment, clinging to each other.

They lay on the lounge very still, neither speaking, listening to the sounds of the waves slapping against the shore below and the beating of their hearts. The Hawaiian jagged waves seem to be speaking to her and telling her it was time to quiet her inner turmoil. Accept Paul and the love he was offering.

"My desire for you surprises me." She leaned up to kiss him.

He held the kiss, and with a husky voice answered, "You can desire me all you want," and gently closed his mouth over hers.

After a long moment of intimate kissing, Meredith rose and walked inside. She realized she was naked, and not the least bit embarrassed knowing Paul was watching her walk to the bedroom. He must like my body, she thought, but I will start going to the gym tomorrow.

They each showered and climbed into bed. Paul encircled Meredith in his arms much like Alex would have done after lovemaking, kissed her goodnight, and in a few minutes, both were sound asleep.

Just before she nodded off, Meredith realized they had never made love in a real bed, but like Scarlett O'Hara—she would think about that tomorrow, as *tomorrow is another day*.

The next few days were lazy and fun. Paul gave Jake the rest of the week off and hired a car and driver to show them around the island. They drove through the Pali Tunnel to Hawaii Kai, Kailua, and out to Pyramid Rock. They had lunch at Roy's Beach House at the Turtle Bay Resort and their table sat right on the beach in the sand. Perfect weather, perfect drive, for a perfect couple.

The following day they went to the Leeward Shore, driving past the USS Arizona Memorial up to the North Shore and watched the young men and women ride the big waves.

They were playing tourist and Meredith knew it was a first for Paul. He had not taken many business calls, which surprised her, and she knew he was trying to make their time on the island a true lover's holiday. He guaranteed her there were others to handle things at the offices. She also knew from his many comments, it had been years since he had taken any time away from his busy career.

Their last night in Honolulu, Paul surprised her with dinner at Michel's at the Colony Surf Hotel. She had casually mentioned a few days earlier it was her favorite restaurant on the island and bragged about their wonderful Lobster Bisque ala Michel's, the signature dish of the restaurant.

As the cab entered the hotel driveway, she hugged Paul and thanked him for the wonderful surprise. Their table was set on the sand and the beautiful lights of the city glowed in the background. When the waiter approached to take their cocktail order Meredith asked if they still served the infamous Green Flash she remembered. Paul laughed and said he had never heard of such a cocktail.

"You've never watched for the green flash over the ocean?" she asked.

He laughed, reached for her hand, and together they looked skyward, each searching for the aurora borealis, also known as the green flash.

They savored a marvelous meal of Kunoa Beef with Truffle Madeira wine sauce served over risotto laced with asparagus that was done flawlessly. Paul enjoyed it so much he mentioned he would ask his chef to add the dish to his personal menu.

They shared a Chocolate Souffle ala Michel's and Meredith knew she should walk all the way back to the Village. She vowed to start a diet when she got back to Coronado.

Their last night they clung to each other on their make-believe terrace dance floor and made the most passionate love of their trip in the sumptuous king-size bed. They felt shut away from the world, both knowing it would soon be time to leave this wonderful paradise and get back to reality.

They packed the next morning, both quiet and sad to be leaving, but Paul quickly reminded her, "We still have our friendly skies."

"Yes, our friendly skies, five grown children, and a few grandchildren. The last few days we have shut everything out, and now it's time to get back to reality."

The children flashed in her mind for the first time since she boarded Paul's private jet in San Diego. What will they think of my having an affair with an old boyfriend? She hoped, no, she knew, they would be happy for her. Would Paul's two sons accept her as the woman their father loved? Secretly, she made herself a promise to bring them all together as one family.

When they arrived at the airport, the RCC corporate jet sat waiting for them. Jake was standing at the foot of the ramp and smiled a look of approval as he gave her a friendly nod.

They ascended the stairs of the massive 737 and Meredith again wanted to pinch herself. By the time they were airborne, it was time for lunch and after they settled in for the five-hour flight, Paul's chef prepared a lunch of poached salmon and fresh vegetables. He surprised Meredith, who was anticipating one of his fancy and very fattening desserts, by serving a small plate of what he touted as warm low-cal chocolate chip cookies.

He was happy for his employer and longtime friend, who even with all his wealth, had no one to share his fabulous lifestyle with. He knew this gracious lady was just the ticket for Mr. Paul. He watched as Paul reached across the table for Meredith's hand and could see the love in the eyes of the wonderful couple. He didn't hear Paul whisper to Meredith it was now time for their favorite kind of dessert.

They rose together, neither one shy, and walked arm-in-arm into the airplane's bedroom. They remained dressed and laid down on the plane's master bed together, knowing their wonderful interlude was about to end. Both wanted the plane to fly forever.

Paul closed his eyes remembering the day on the river's edge and confessed to Meredith how he had wanted to run after her so much he hurt inside. "I can still remember helping you into your car and watching you drive away. I never want to lose you again. Can you find a place in your heart for me? I love you and want to marry you."

Meredith was surprised by his words. Marriage was a big step at their age.

"We have children and grandchildren to consider. I would like them to get to know us as a couple before we make such an announcement, especially considering how short a time it's been since we found each other again."

Although he understood her hesitation, Paul didn't want to waste another minute for their lives together to begin. But he would do his best to give her the time and space she needed. He pulled her close to him, gently kissed her, and closed his eyes.

As they were preparing to take their seats for landing, Paul took a deep breath. "Once I see you home, I have to leave for Washington. My government associates have planned a meeting I must attend. I don't want to leave you, but I must. I'm sorry."

"I understand, Paul, and of course you must go," she added.

Paul was thankful she did not question him, as he could not reveal the extent of his government involvement, concerned it could jeopardize his cover. He was a contractor, but the roads he built now led to intelligence and information highways for his confidential contacts around the world. His life was a spider's web of secrets.

They were quiet on the descent into San Diego, both knowing they would prefer to stay in their friendly skies. Earth and reality were getting closer by the minute.

Upon their arrival at the executive terminal, Jake helped with the bags and drove the waiting town car to The Shores. Passing over the Coronado Bridge, Meredith was the first to break the silence. She took Paul's hand, "I will miss you," she said quietly, trying hard to control the sadness in her voice.

They pulled into the roundabout of the El Cortez building and the doorman rushed to greet them. As they walked into the building, neither noticed the gardener watching them, his hat pulled down and sunglasses covering most of his face. To them, he looked like any other Shores employee. Meredith paid little attention but later wished she had.

Jeffery had been waiting for Meredith to return and was disappointed to see she wasn't alone. He watched the man pick up her bags and enter the building with her. Would he stay?

Paul carried her bags and they entered the elevator in silence. He helped her with the door key and once inside her apartment encircled her in his arms.

As they held each other tears burned her eyes. "I don't know why I am crying. This has been a most wonderful week. I will remember it for the rest of my life. You best go before I beg you to stay."

"Beg me, please."

"Oh Paul, it's off you go to your big meeting and we'll talk tomorrow."

"I will call you later to say good night," and then he kissed her. He wanted to stay in her arms all night, but he had to get to DC. They stood in the doorway like teenagers each not wanting to leave the other.

Meredith watched him walk down the hall to the elevator and was awestruck by his physical resemblance to Alex. She had said goodbye to her husband many times, yet this time, the goodbye was to a lover. Imagine, me having a lover, and with a smile, she turned, closed, and locked the door.

Sighing, she walked towards her bedroom. Her life had been turned upside down in a matter of weeks. She had slept with a man she hardly knew, even if he was an old friend, and she had enjoyed it. What would her children and friends think?

She had undressed and just sat down on the bed when the phone rang. She picked up the portable receiver and found no one there. Oh, she thought, must have been a wrong number. She could never imagine someone would be checking to see if she was home, someone watching her and waiting to do her harm.

When the phone rang again, she picked it up and the cheery voice was her darling Jennifer, making sure "Mom was home and had a good time." She wanted to hear all about the trip. "Why have I not heard from you the entire time you have been away?"

Meredith briefly explained her trip but left out many of the details including the private jet and moonlight swim.

Jen was quick to say she had also been busy and had gone to San Francisco for a business meeting with Stan, so they were even. For the first time in years, they hadn't known where the other was. Jennifer was interrupted by Stan telling them they were late for a dinner date with friends, so she wished her mother a restful night and was off the line.

Good, a reprieve, thought Meredith. Even at the early hour of eight p.m., she crawled into bed. She tried to read the book she had been carrying around for weeks to help herself relax, but thoughts of Paul and all the excitement of the last few days, their trip, and passionate lovemaking, made concentrating impossible.

She ran her hand over the soft sheet and wished Paul was there beside her. Not just to make love to her, even though that would be wonderful, but to be near her. She wondered where he was, and if he was thinking of her.

Just then the phone rang again. Who could it be this time? She was greeted with a, "Hello, my darling Sunshine."

"Oh Paul, I was hoping you would call."

"I wish I was there beside you," he said.

"You are and I miss you so."

"I miss you, too," Paul replied.

They talked for almost an hour and it amazed Meredith knowing they were able to do so when he was in the air on his way to DC. "Your voice through the airplane phone is so clear it sounds like you are just down the hall."

"Oh, keep teasing me and I will turn this plane around and come get you. The skies are very lonely tonight."

They discussed social events, the upcoming Christmas holidays, and Paul even mentioned retirement, shocking her slightly. "You know I am of that age when many men are retired. Just think of all the fun we could have. We could find a new place to make love every night."

"I think the thin air is getting to you," Meredith laughed. "I think it's time for both of us to get some sleep."

"Would you meet me in Chicago next weekend?" he asked. "I have to give a speech for the National Association of Contractors. It's a black-tie event. I would love a date and even more for the weekend event if you are willing."

Meredith laughed, and said, "I would love to be your date, and yes, I am willing."

Paul told her, "I will send Jake for you on Friday." She promised she would be ready and waiting.

CHAPTER 13

Meredith spent the week getting packed *again*. She even pampered herself with one of those wonderful massages she had begun to enjoy.

In typical girl fashion, she had saved one little black dress, a bit old, but very flattering, and classic enough to escort the guest of honor to his big event. The Coronado sun was out every afternoon, and she kept a close check on her tan. She even managed a couple of days on the bicycle machine in the exercise room at the complex.

Jake arrived promptly at 9 a.m. Friday morning. They drove to the private terminal of the San Diego Airport, where, surprisingly, a different RCC jet was waiting for them. As Meredith boarded, she noticed it was called a Gulfstream *something* and was smaller than the one they traveled in for their trip to Hawaii. How many airplanes did Paul's company own?

As she settled herself in the cabin, Meredith thought of the conversation she had with Jennifer the day before. She told her an old friend had asked her to accompany him to an event in Chicago and had offered to fly her there if she could stay the weekend. She hadn't mentioned the private jet with all the trimmings, or the shared hotel suite. She didn't

167

consider it lying ... just not telling the entire truth.

Jen was thrilled and said, "Mom, it's the perfect thing for you to do." She didn't ask too many questions, and for once Meredith was glad Jen was too busy to get inquisitive.

A town car was waiting when they landed at O'Hare's private executive terminal, but still, there was no sign of Paul.

It had been many years since she had been to Chicago and the sounds of big-city excitement were everywhere. She wondered where Jake was taking her but already decided not to ask questions, as Paul's life seemed full of surprises.

Jake drove her to a boutique hotel, small by Chicago standards, located just off Michigan Avenue. Meredith noticed Neiman Marcus on the corner just outside the door of the hotel and although shopping wasn't her big thing anymore, she loved to browse their windows and take a peek at Neiman's china department. She hoped for a free hour or two just to enjoy walking through the beautiful store. It was like going to Market for all the gift merchandise she bought for her retail stores for so many years. If it showed on a Neiman Marcus shelf, she knew she had made an excellent selection.

The hotel was no Hilton Hawaiian Village in size, but when the bellman opened the double doors to the suite she was taken back by the beauty of the room. A large bouquet of yellow roses sat on the entry table. The attached note read simply *To My Love*. How could he have guessed yellow roses were her favorite flower?

Seeing her reaction Jake excused himself. "Please

get settled, ma'am. I am sure Mr. Paul will be arriving soon." When she turned, he was gone.

She walked into the bedroom and stood looking in amazement at the bed.

There were yellow rose petals sprinkled over the bed and a note on the pillow. As she opened the card her hands were trembling. *Until tonight, my darling.* Clutching the card to her breast she wondered just how she was so lucky to have found this wonderful romantic man.

Meredith unpacked her suitcase and hung her simple black dress in the closet after ensuring it had traveled well. She had used her famous tissue paper trick and felt it was ready to wear. She kicked off her shoes, stretched out on the sofa, and drifted off to sleep.

It was nearing four when she woke but as of yet, she had not heard a word from Paul. She knew he would be arriving soon, so after a warm relaxing bath, she dressed, applied her makeup, and slipped into her cocktail dress. She admired herself in the full-length mirror as she attached the beautiful diamond necklace Paul had given her in Hawaii. She knew she looked stunning, but where was the guest of honor?

Meredith walked to the veranda a bit nervous. The view of the skyscrapers in the distance was spectacular. She had not heard the door open and then from behind her a deep voice asked, "Are you enjoying the view?"

As she turned there stood a new Paul. He was dressed in a black tuxedo and looked so handsome she wanted to cry. He opened his arms and she walked into them. They kissed and clung to each other.

"I have missed you so," he said in a husky voice that made her shiver down to her toes. Pushing her back, he admired her slim figure in the stylish evening dress. "You look lovely."

"If I am in a dream, don't wake me," she added, as she felt his eyes scan her body.

"I have a gift for you," Paul said and from his pocket produced a small white box tied with a gold ribbon. "I bought you a little trinket to wear tonight. I hope you will accept it with my deepest love."

He placed the box in her hand. Meredith untied the ribbon and gasped. Quailed in the tiny box was a baguette diamond bracelet, her favorite cut of diamonds. How could he have known?

"Oh," she exclaimed, "It's gorgeous! But Paul—"

"But Paul, what?" he responded. "Let me help you with the clasp."

"How can I thank you?" she said as she placed a light kiss on his cheek.

Paul was quick to reply he would find a way when they returned.

Jake knocked and then opened the door. "Mr. Paul, we must be going or we'll be late. The banquet starts in thirty minutes."

"We'll have to continue this later," Paul said, as he took her by the arm and led her to the open elevator.

Jake drove them to the Waldorf Astoria near Michigan Avenue. Paul seemed relaxed as he rode to the hotel holding Meredith's hand. He told her about Margaret Parker, his executive assistant, and all-around girl Friday. She had worked for him for fifteen years and was one of the best speechwriters in the business. "I hope she doesn't let me down in front of my best girl."

The hotel was a blaze of lights. They entered the vast lobby and were immediately swept away to the ballroom by two of the evening's organizers who were waiting for the guest speaker's arrival. As they entered the large banquet room Meredith suddenly realized the importance of the man at her side. They were greeted by many well-wishers and then ushered to the dais where she was seated next to Paul.

Following dinner, the Mayor of Chicago spoke briefly. The President of the National Contractors Association, John Anderson, then introduced Paul as the keynote speaker.

Paul's resume surprised Meredith. She had no idea of his impressive background. He had obtained a Master of Business from the McDonough School of Business at Georgetown University in Washington, DC. Why had he not included that impressive milestone when they had discussed their pasts over the last few weeks? One more piece to his secret puzzle. Did his connection with Washington come about because of the time he spent at McDonough?

Paul took his place in front of the microphone. He didn't look toward Meredith as he spoke, afraid he might lose his train of thought. When he finished his comments on International Contract Law and Finance, Meredith wanted to stand up and cheer. He was an eloquent speaker and charmed his audience, as well as her. When the applause died down, he casually walked towards Meredith. She wanted to rush to his arms but kept herself poised, pleased when he reached for her hand as he sat down.

"You were wonderful," she whispered to him. "I am so impressed."

A short closing speech was given, and then guests began departing the banquet room. Meredith and Paul tried to exit the ballroom but were stopped many times by his numerous friends. A quick drive to their hotel and they were finally alone, standing in yet another elevator.

"We seem to spend a lot of time in elevators," she laughed. "I was so proud of you tonight." She flung herself into his arms and kissed him hard. Breathless she added, in her most seductive voice, "Mrs. Parker's speech materials were excellent and your delivery was outstanding."

"If my public speaking impresses you, wait until you see my presentation and delivery in the bedroom."

Meredith tugged at his arm and they both were laughing as the elevator door opened.

"I can't believe we both came from such humble beginnings, and here we stand in this beautiful suite. Next, they will want you to run for public office."

"Oh, they asked me," he joked.

"I bet, and just what did you say in response."

"I said I didn't have a first lady." He turned and kissed her with gentle passion.

"Here we are, acting like teenagers again," she said when they moved apart.

As they walked towards the bedroom, she had to ask what she most dreaded, "When do you leave again?"

"In the morning around 7 a.m.," he replied. "I wish I could take you with me."

As they entered the bedroom Paul's cell phone rang. Recognizing the number, he answered, listened, and announced he needed to take the call. As Meredith watched his expression change, she knew something was wrong.

"I'm sorry," he said as he ended the call, "but I must leave."

"Now?!" Her voice sounded shocked and disappointed.

"Yes, I have an emergency. I must get back to DC as soon as possible. Jake keeps the plane ready at all times for situations such as this. I will send him back for you after he drops me off."

Meredith couldn't believe it. She said, almost pleading, "Can't I go with you?"

"No. I am afraid not. I'm so sorry. I promise to make it up to you as soon as this situation is resolved. You know I would love to have you in the friendly skies with me tonight, but I can't this time."

Meredith didn't know what to say. She stood there in a beautiful hotel suite, in her only black dress, wearing diamonds, yet being treated like a mistress, a mistress to his work.

She was determined to make it easy for him to leave, but as she raised her head and looked into his eyes her tears began falling. He reached for her and she clung to him. Paul sensed her inner confusion and held her tenderly as he would a wounded child.

"Someday, my darling, you will understand. How about a trip to Palm Springs next weekend so I can meet your daughter? We can even plan a trip to meet

173

my sons."

"Sounds wonderful," she assured him through her tears, "but I will have to stay with Jennifer and Stan, and you will have to stay in a hotel."

"Do I have to?" he laughingly whined.

"Yes, you do."

"We do? I thought with age came privilege."

"Paul, what would she think if she knew we were here alone?"

"I hope she would be happy her mother had found a man who loves her with all his heart."

He kissed her passionately. Paul knew if he didn't leave right away, they would end up on the rose petals. As much as it pained him to leave her, his duty was to his country and the President of the United States.

As he released her, she looked into his eyes. "Should I stay here at the hotel and wait for you until you finish your business in Washington?"

"No, try and get a good night's sleep. I will send Jake for you around noon tomorrow."

They walked to the door arm in arm, neither wanting to let go. "I love you, Meredith Evans."

"Oh Paul, I love you too," she replied, and in a moment, he was gone.

Meredith turned to walk back to the bedroom where she would now sleep alone. She undressed, reached for her favorite silk nightgown but instead put it back. A soft terry robe supplied by the hotel looked much more comforting. It would keep her warm, she thought. Paul had left, who would see her anyway?

She laid her head on the pillow and reached across to caress the other side where he should be. She had thought sexual thrills would never be hers again, then along came Paul.

But tonight there was no Paul, and once again she lay in bed alone.

CHAPTER 14

As Paul reluctantly released Meredith and walked towards the door he was already dialing Jake. Once he was on the line, Paul told him to begin preparing the jet for an immediate departure.

Jake questioned whether Paul needed a ride to the airport, and was told, "No, just take care of the plane. I'll find my way to the airport."

Walking briskly from the hotel, Paul was able to flag down a taxi that had just dropped off passengers and directed the driver to the executive terminal at O'Hare International. Once the taxi was moving, he leaned back and sighed for the woman he had left teary-eyed and heartbroken as he rushed away from her with no explanation.

He was determined to marry her and knew to do that he had to make a definite change in his life.

Paul's construction company had been a major vendor for the federal government since the mid-eighties. At the time, in addition to major projects in Las Vegas, Richardson Construction Company focused on government contracts in and around New Mexico. A full-service construction company, RCC handled anything needed by private industry and government agencies. To employ the best talent, the human resources team recruited from engineering and technology-heavy universities and was also known to entice top-notch executives from other companies.

The company opened offices in DC in 1992 and soon all of RCC's local projects were related to the government in one way or another. Within a year, Paul was approached by the State Department with a surprising proposal. Would he consider accepting occasional secret projects from the government using RCC as his cover, essentially, become a covert agent? During the meeting with State Department officials, Paul was amazed to hear how much they knew of his life. From birth to his time in the Marines to the present day, they knew everything.

The Department representatives explained he would not be a formal government employee but would have top-secret clearance, which meant he could not share his assignments with anyone—even his family or others within his company. All requests from the government would be his top priority, even if they conflicted with an RCC contracted task. When he was on a State Department assignment, whether it was domestic or international, his company would take a back seat other than providing his cover.

He asked if he would be required to carry a weapon and was told it would depend on the mission. Although he had been a Marine and completed a tour of Vietnam in the sixties, Paul knew he would need re-training with newer weapons. He was told he would also be expected to learn more about intelligence gathering and foreign diplomacy.

178

Understanding the proposition was a total surprise, but in need of reliable operatives, the officials asked Paul to give them his answer within forty-eight hours. He did not need that long to accept the challenge.

When the September 11, 2001 attacks rocked the country, RCC was one of many companies the military reached out to for help rebuilding the damaged Pentagon since Paul and his crews had already passed the extensive background checks required to work on federal projects.

RCC committed to the very aggressive timeline established by The Phoenix Project, the group tasked with ensuring the destroyed wing of the Pentagon was ready to be re-occupied within a year of the bombing. Thanks to round-the-clock shifts, exterior work was substantially completed twenty-eight days ahead of schedule. One of Paul's proudest moments as a builder was watching that final piece of limestone, still stained and marred from the impact of the plane, be set into place.

Jake had everything ready for departure when the taxi dropped Paul off at the terminal. All he needed was to file the final flight plan. Within the hour he had the plane in the air, heading for Paul's next assignment, locating and rescuing a kidnapped US Ambassador in Turkey.

"You only need to get me to DC. From there I will be taking a military plane to Turkey," Paul told him. "Then I need you to return here by noon tomorrow and ensure Meredith arrives home safely."

Paul walked out to the living room of the plane and Jake appeared from the galley carrying two mugs of hot coffee. They sat together for the first time in a few days and Jake knew his friend was deep in thought. "Things will be fine when we get you to DC, Boss," Jake said.

"I want out of this war," Paul blurted. "It's not my war. We have both seen so much in our years together. I have finally found the love of my life and I want her back. I want out."

Paul turned to Jake, "Wouldn't you like someone in your life too? Someone to come home to and love?"

Jake nodded. "Yes, at times I know what I'm missing. I keep one eye open for the right woman, but she will have to dazzle me right out of my pilot's seat. I want an exciting, gorgeous woman who will want me as much as I desire her. Not a lot to ask, right?"

Paul looked at his old friend and said, "Jake, you've earned a wonderful life. Let's hope you find her soon." They toasted each other with their coffee mugs to a life with less stress and government responsibility, and more love.

Paul had met Jake Skyler when they were serving as Marines during the Vietnam conflicts in the sixties. He had enlisted while Jake had been drafted. They were two young men from Phoenix dropped into a gruesome situation which neither speaks of today. Both felt lucky they made it home, unlike the close to sixty thousand US soldiers who perished.

During one of the lengthy and deadly battles of 1968, Paul found Jake lying in a ditch and carried him to safety, Jake barely alive following a mortar attack. Doctors were able to patch him up physically, but his mental state was destroyed. Like many other young men and women, they survived the horrible war, but the bloody conflicts, drugs, and Viet Cong made for years of nightmares that altered their lives.

Paul went back to his family in the States and dove into his new construction company. Jake took to the streets. Paul lost track of his fellow Vietnam soldier until he noticed an article in the local newspaper regarding the arrest of a man awaiting trial in a Phoenix jail for disorderly conduct. Looking closer, Paul thought he recognized the bearded face of his old war buddy. He went to the police station for details and confirmed his suspicions. Jake was homeless, on the streets, and accused of fighting with another indigent person under a freeway bridge.

He requested a visit with Jake at the jail and was shocked at the condition of his old friend. Jake's hair was long and shaggy, his beard was starting to gray, and it was obvious the drinking and drugs had taken him to a very dark place.

"I wish you had left me in that ditch in Nam to die. I can't sleep, can't hold a job, and the nightmares of what we saw there still plague me."

Paul was unsettled by Jake's admission. He had run into other military buddies since the war, even hired a few to work on his construction crews. He had helped others and couldn't bear to see his friend so alone and without hope in the prime of his life.

"I don't know if you remember me talking about wanting to start my own construction company when we were in Nam. I followed through with that and it's doing well. I could use someone like you. Of course, you have some work to do on yourself first, but I am willing to help. What do you say?"

Jake was humbled by Paul's suggestion. "You know I have nothing to offer you, but I know how to work hard when given a chance, and would do my best. It might take me a bit of time to get clean. Are you willing to hold the job for me?"

"Yes, if you get clean and stay clean. I am also prepared to help financially if you need it until you get back on your feet. And don't worry, I'll keep you busy."

"I can't believe this. Thanks, man! I accept. What do you think I need to do next?"

"Let me look into it. I will see you again soon," Paul said.

He bailed Jake out of jail and checked him into a rehab facility. Paul was truly impressed by Jake's determination to rebuild not only his habits but his body as well. When Jake emerged from rehab, Paul was amazed at the change in his old friend. He had bulked up, was well-groomed, had a spark again, and enthusiastically shook Paul's hand in thanks.

"I'm ready to work," Jake said with a grateful smile.

"Then let's get to it," Paul responded. "You drive."

Jake's life took a new path. He soon became

Paul's driver and go-to guy for a wide assortment of jobs. For the first time in his life, someone trusted him completely.

The first few years after joining Richardson Construction Company, they seemed to be on the road constantly with Jake always behind the wheel everywhere they went. When the trip was out of town, he was responsible for arranging for transportation and ensuring Paul got where he needed to be safely and on time.

About five years into his time with RCC, the company invested in their first private plane, a small Gulfstream. Paul asked if Jake was interested in learning to fly and he jumped at the chance since that had been one of his biggest dreams. Paul arranged for him to attend flight training school in Phoenix. Once certified for the Gulfstream, going from job to job became faster for the pair. When Paul decided to add a 737 to his growing fleet, Jake went back to flight school to earn his certification for the new plane.

One of the few things not going Jake's way was his personal life, which was basically nil. He had stayed in touch with very few of his old friends and even after he cleaned himself up, had a hard time trusting a new acquaintance enough to call them *friend*.

Women were attracted to his good looks and strong build, but there was a dark side to him only Paul seemed to understand. After meeting Paul's wife and sons, and in occasional conversations with Paul, Jake would say he hoped to one day meet a special woman but had yet to find one who held his interest for more than a couple of dates.

He craved excitement and living on the edge, which made him curious about Paul's unexplained side trips. Jake often tried to extract an answer from his friend but Paul remained tight-lipped about his solo excursions. Selfishly, Paul knew it would be great to have a close confidant to discuss some of his classified missions with. So he took the idea to his State Department handlers.

As soon as Jake heard the Department's proposition he accepted, excited to become a part of that hush-hush world. His previous experience with the military had been tough, but no longer the broken man who had returned from Vietnam, Jake loved his country and was ready to offer his services wherever needed. After completing the approval process and receiving the proper clearances, he was allowed to attend briefings and accompany Paul on most of his government trips, piloting the corporate jet when necessary.

Paul knew Jake always had his back and vice versa. He was strong, quiet, and dedicated to the man he now called *Mr. Paul*. Their secrets were safe with each other and that's the way things would stay.

CHAPTER 15

When Meredith awoke the next morning, her first thoughts were of Paul—where was he, who was he, and why did he seem to have so many secrets. She was still heartbroken over the way he rushed away from her and their romantic weekend after the mysterious phone call. Who was on the other end of that call? What was so important he felt it was acceptable to bolt out the door, leaving her alone and with no idea where he was going? The more she stewed, the more hurt she became and she felt a sudden need to slow down their love affair until she understood more about his life.

If he truly loved her why couldn't he confide in her? She realized their relationship was still relatively new, but she needed some explanations from Paul before continuing further and was bound and determined to get them. Maybe next week in Palm Springs she could convince him to open up to her about his life and explain his vanishing acts. Her heart ached with the possibility they might be over before really beginning again, but she had to be honest with herself and her feelings.

Packed and dressed in her comfortable traveling clothes, Meredith added the beautiful new bracelet from Paul to her wrist along with her usual set of gold bangles. Then she sat and waited for Jake to appear to take her to the airport. "I feel like a kept woman," she heard herself say out loud, a phrase she and Alex had often laughed about over their forty years of marriage. She was beginning to wonder if the same was true again.

The flight back to California was quiet for Meredith. The crew was polite and attentive, but Meredith stayed to herself, feeling uncomfortable on board the corporate jet without Paul. She tried to read the same book she had taken to both DC and Hawaii but couldn't keep her eyes focused on the page. Her mind kept drifting to the interrupted weekend and she found herself relating her unfinished book to her life these days. So many questions with no impending answers.

After a smooth landing in San Diego, she was ushered to the waiting town car and before she knew it, Jake was driving her to the island.

When he pulled up in the large circle of her tower, they both failed to see the man pretending to be gardening to the right side of the driveway. Employees were usually gone by mid-afternoon.

Once again Jeffery Sanders went unnoticed.

Meredith walked towards the building where Ralph, the day man, was holding the large glass door open, Jake following her with the bags. She started to take them from him, but was told, "Mr. Paul instructed me to see you home and that means to your door."

She entered her condo with Jake close behind her and was greeted by a large bouquet of yellow roses on the coffee table. "How does he do all these things,

Jake?"

He smiled and said, "He calls his personal shopper, Margaret Parker. Ma'am, I think he loves you very much."

"Oh, Jake, I hope so," Meredith replied.

Jake extended his hand, and although Meredith wanted to give him a hug she shook his hand instead. There would be time for closeness later.

As he left the condo he said, "I will see you in Palm Springs ma'am," and she had no doubt he would be there with Mr. Paul.

Meredith walked over to the flowers and read the card. *Until next weekend. All my love, Paul.* She clutched the card and wanted to cry, but she had shed enough tears these past three years for a lifetime. Even with her indecision regarding their relationship, she chose to smile and thank heaven above for her luck in finding such a wonderful man to love.

Unpacking her carry-on she found the small white box with the gold ribbon that had contained the beautiful gift from Paul now sparkling on her wrist. Who gives diamond bracelets so early in a relationship, and what kind of women accept them? Very rich men give them to their mistress, was her only answer. Is that what I am? The question spun around and around in her head.

Meredith tried to sleep in the next morning and woke at eight. Bolstered by two cups of strong coffee, she picked up the phone to call Jennifer. She needed her closest friend, and that had always been her daughter. She told her about the wonderful trip to Chicago. She explained how interesting and important her friend's speech had been. She conveniently left out the part about the private jet, the posh hotel suite, and the diamond bracelet.

Jen was quick to imagine her mother in the arms of a gigolo and warned her to be careful, but Jennifer was warning her mother to be cautious of the wrong man. She could not have imagined what another desperate man had in mind for Meredith.

They both agreed to the upcoming weekend and Jennifer was pleased her mother wanted to introduce them to the gentleman she had met in Washington, DC. They planned dinner at the country club, and a golf outing if Paul played.

After ending the call, Meredith sat staring at nothing. There was so much she didn't know about this puzzling man who had come back into her life. The man who had received a mysterious phone call during their romantic weekend and rushed away, leaving her alone in a Chicago hotel room.

Thursday afternoon Jake called for Mr. Paul. "Do you need transportation to Palm Springs, Mrs. Meredith?" he questioned.

"No, thanks, Jake," she replied. "I need my car when I get there. I am driving over tomorrow." She was starting to have doubts Paul would get away to make the trip and hoped he would at least arrive by Saturday for dinner. Meredith knew Paul had her cell number, but just in case she gave Jen's home and office numbers for Jake to add to his list of telephone numbers Paul might need.

Jake knew by the tone of her voice she had not heard from Paul and was unsure himself if Mr. Paul could break free and get to Palm Springs for the weekend. He hoped Mrs. Meredith would not end up disappointed again.

CHAPTER 16

Meredith planned to be on the road to the desert by 10 a.m. the next morning. She was parked in the underground garage unaware once again she was being watched by Jeffery Sanders.

She had only one small suitcase to pull, her make-up case to carry, and a purse slung over her shoulder as she always left clothes hanging in Jen's closet in case she made an unexpected trip to the desert. Her condo was a quick three-hour drive to Jen's home in Indian Wells and with the new wider freeway, she always felt comfortable behind the wheel of her large SUV.

Leaving later in the morning to avoid the work traffic, she didn't notice the dark sedan following a few car lengths behind. But he was there, stalking her as he had for many months.

As she listened to her favorite radio station she made the turn off Interstate 15 onto Highway 74. She had traveled the mountain road many times and was aware of its many dangerous twists and turns, but it shortened the trip to Palm Springs by forty minutes and she always drove at a guarded speed.

Glancing into her rearview mirror as she neared the summit, she saw a car had crept up much too close behind her. Since there was no passing lane, she pulled over as far as she safely could. Hugging the right side of the highway and slowing down a bit, Meredith expected the driver to take advantage of the additional room on the road and sail by. But as she moved over so did the car behind her.

Suddenly she realized the driver had crept up even closer behind her and seemed almost on her bumper. She flashed her brakes to get him to back away. But instead of falling back he abruptly pulled to the left as if to pass her. As his car came up beside her, the driver swerved sharply towards her. Meredith screamed and pulled the wheel slightly more to the right to avoid a collision, horrified as she moved ever closer to the edge of the cliff. Glancing at the car next to her, Meredith had a sick feeling the driver was preparing to attempt slamming into her car again.

Terrified, she looked ahead and realized she was very near the turn-off to the Indian casino. She saw a straight spot in the road, put her foot hard on the gas pedal, and pressed it to the floor. The large SUV responded and lurched forward.

She spun wildly into the casino entrance driveway, almost colliding with their sign and barely missing two parked cars. She quickly brought the car to a stop and with shaky hands grabbed her keys and purse, and raced to the security guard standing at the door. She didn't even take a minute to glance over her shoulder to see if the man with the hat hiding his eyes had followed her into the parking lot.

Having noticed her dramatic entrance into the parking lot and her look of distress, the guard called for backup as he helped Meredith to the casino manager's office. Once there, she found a quiet corner and tried to gain control of herself. Sobbing, she called Jennifer to tell her what had happened, but all she was able to force out was her location.

"Stay put Mom, have a drink to calm your nerves. Stan and I will be there as soon as possible."

She knew she was too upset to even attempt to drive the rest of the way by herself, so she thanked her daughter, and tried to compose herself.

The town of Anza, located in the mountains near Temecula, and the casino run by the Cahuilla Indians, is literally in the middle of nowhere, but within a few minutes, the Tribal police had arrived. She tried to describe the car but since her main concern was not driving over the cliff, she could only remember the color. And even though she had briefly glanced at the man, the hat and dark glasses he wore made any identification impossible.

She was still shaken when Jennifer and Stan arrived more than an hour later. "Why would someone try and hurt me," she wept. "He tried to run me off the road and almost pushed me over the cliff."

While Jennifer stayed with her mother, Stan took immediate charge of the situation and spoke to the police about the incident. With so little to go on, the officers felt it was a random event, but would keep the situation under investigation.

With nothing more anyone could do at the time, Stan ushered Meredith and Jen to his waiting Range Rover. "I'll drive your car and follow the two of you home."

Meredith asked Stan to call her friend Paul and tell him of her situation as he would soon be on his way to Palm Springs. She handed him a business card and Stan gazed at the last name in amazement. Did Meredith have any idea who this man was?

Jennifer drove slowly while her mother rested in the passenger seat, trying to relax. Meredith eventually closed her eyes and slept. Who could be so cruel to the lovely lady seated beside her?

Once behind the gates of Verrado Country Club, Meredith finally felt safe. After a strong cocktail on the patio, Jennifer helped her mother settle in one of the guest rooms. Meredith was asleep in minutes, dreaming she was in the safety of Paul's strong arms.

Jen went back later to check on her mother and seeing her lying there asleep, so small and fragile, made her realize just how vulnerable Meredith was. Jennifer had always felt that even living alone, the security at the beach would keep her mother safe. As they now knew, nothing would keep some crazy person from trying to harm her away from the beach. But for what reason?

As she pulled the door of Meredith's bedroom closed, Jennifer heard Stan talking on the phone and assumed he had reached her mother's friend, Paul. She heard Stan say Meredith was with them and resting quietly. Jennifer listened as Stan relayed the details as he knew them.

Shocked, Paul answered that his plane was currently returning from London and would be arriving in Palm Springs in the morning.

"Please tell her I am on my way, and not to worry. Reassure her I will take care of the situation."

Jen asked for the phone and he repeated his

comments to her. She was quick to add they were both quite capable of taking care of her mother.

"I am sure you are, Jennifer. I look forward to meeting you and Stan."

Very smooth, Jen thought. She was anxious to meet this new man in her mother's life. Stan was right though, he sounded like a force to be reckoned with.

The large RCC 737 with Jake at the controls landed at the Executive Terminal of the Palm Springs Airport the following morning at 8 a.m. Paul had tried to sleep on the trip home from Europe but was restless and worried about Meredith, and he arrived stressed.

Who would try and hurt a woman like Meredith and why? Paul knew he would move heaven and earth to find this crazed person and punish him. More importantly, what in the world was *he* doing in London when Meredith needed him? His answer was company business and his concern was what Meredith would think when she found out just what company he worked for. He thought of his secret life, and how it might affect her. Did someone try to get to him by hurting Meredith? He had made many enemies in his career. He had to get to the bottom of this attack on her immediately.

After landing, Jake drove him towards Indian Wells. Jennifer had been very specific he arrive near 9 a.m., so he asked Jake to take a long route. They drove through the Palm Springs shopping district on Palm Canyon Drive, then about half an hour further to Palm Desert. Paul looked for the stores Meredith had founded so many years before and was impressed by the well-manicured streets lined with beautiful art galleries, colorful flowers, and boutique shops of every kind. He had heard of the area but never taken time to visit. He was always too busy, but that was going to change if Meredith would marry him.

Jennifer had arranged entrance for him into the country club. His car pulled past the large waterfalls lining the drive and up to the security booth where Jake was handed the customary paper pass and they were allowed to enter the club grounds.

The manicured streets and rolling expanse of impeccable lawns flowed onto the beautiful golf course. The entire place was a picture of wealth and status. His homes were all hotels except for his secret retreat in Hawaii. To his surprise, Paul didn't like the show of wealth he was driving through and wondered if Meredith did.

Jake stopped in front of the Barrington home and told Paul, "I'll go to the hotel and check us both in. See you tomorrow, Boss."

Paul rang the doorbell at exactly nine and was greeted by Jennifer and Stan.

"So nice to meet you, Mr. Richardson," Stan said, as he extended his hand. He was quick to ask them to call him Paul.

Jennifer had the rundown on Paul and what an exceptional businessman he was from Stan, and she too graciously offered her hand and welcomed him into their home. Then she led him to her mother who was waiting on the patio.

He followed them through the elegant home, but his eyes were laser-focused on the lady resting on the lounge. When Meredith saw him, she rose and in three steps was in his arms. He could feel her tears on his neck.

"I am so sorry I was not here with you, my love," he whispered. Paul held her gently until she composed herself.

As they watched from the doorway, Jennifer and Stan knew they were looking at two people who were much more than old friends. They walked toward the two of them and everyone joined in a discussion of Meredith's experience. Stan explained to Paul the police felt it was an isolated incident and they had as much information from Meredith as she could give. The sketchy description gave them little to go on but they had promised to continue to work on the case at their local headquarters.

After more than twenty years in his line of work, Paul knew nothing was ever *isolated*. He needed to retire so he could protect Meredith, and live a normal life. When his current project was finished, he promised himself, he would change his occupation.

Stan knew of the world-famous construction magnate and soon both men were engrossed in the world of detective business and high finance, eager to work together to help Meredith remain safe.

After discussing all possible scenarios with the little information they had, Stan and Jen decided to step away for their scheduled 18-holes of golf, especially now that Paul was with Meredith. Before they were completely out the door though, Jennifer stuck her head around the corner and reminded the two that dinner would be at the country club at seven that evening. "See you both later," she said, and with that, she and Stan were off.

Once they were alone, it became very clear just how upset Paul was. He was quick to say, "Meredith, this would not have happened if you had let Jake drive you to Palm Springs."

"I am very capable of driving over the mountain myself," Meredith responded sharply.

"You are unless some nut case tries to run you off the road," he replied.

His actions reminded her she had important topics to discuss with him. But she knew he was afraid of what she had been through and his anxiety for her safety was being expressed in a very sharp tone.

"You're right, and yes, I was terrified," she said as she reached for his hand and encouraged him to sit in the lounge chair beside her. "But I won't become a recluse, hidden away in my home because of one crazy incident. I cannot rely on Jake to be there every time I want to take a road trip."

"I understand what you are saying and I agree that you must be able to live your life, but I'm very upset over what happened, especially since we don't have any clues as to why." He leaned over to her and kissed her gently. "I want you to be safe—I just found you again."

A little later Meredith invited Paul into the kitchen for lunch. "You can help me whip up something. What would you like for lunch?" she added. The twinkle in his eyes told her just what he wanted to whip up.

"You," he replied, with a devilish grin. She smiled in agreement.

Meredith took his hand and led him toward her

guest bedroom. "There are no rose petals this time, just you and me." She reached for him and held his face, kissing him. They entered the room and as his arms encircled her and the kiss deepened, Meredith realized just how much she needed his wonderful exciting touch. Within minutes they were both shedding their clothes.

"Lock the door," she said laughing. "What if the kids come home?"

"We need some real privacy," Paul added, "and I know just the place."

"Well, for now, this place will have to do."

He pulled her down on the bed, kissing her so hard she thought she might break in half. The foreplay they always planned went out the window, again. They moved together like two young lovers, each trying to please the other. As they came together, Meredith quietly whispered his name and held on as if her life depended on him. Little did she know, it did.

"I love you, and I want you as my wife."

When she stopped gasping for breath, she asked, "Is this an indecent proposal?"

"Marry me, please. I want you for the rest of my life."

Meredith snuggled closer to him, and said in her favorite Scarlett O'Hara voice, "I'll think about that tomorrow, Rhett." He hugged her tighter and they both laughed.

They dressed and headed to the kitchen. When Meredith asked where he would like his lunch served, the patio or the kitchen, he promptly answered, "How about the bedroom?"

"You are insatiable," laughed Meredith.

Paul walked up behind her and kissed her on the neck.

"I am making up for the last forty years. I don't want to waste another minute."

Meredith knew he loved her but was she ready for marriage at her stage in life? And what about his secrets? She had many things to consider before giving him an answer to that particular question and quickly changed the subject.

Returning to the kitchen, Meredith made sandwiches. Paul picked up the tray and they headed for the beautiful covered patio. They enjoyed the afternoon together, and when Jennifer and Stan returned from their round of golf, Meredith and Paul were sitting in the same place where they had left them earlier. Jennifer wondered whether they had moved at all. Would she be surprised to learn the truth?

Dinner that evening at the country club dining room was perfect. When a small combo began to play Paul asked Meredith to dance. Jennifer was pleased with her mother's acceptance.

She stared at her mother in the arms of another man. A bit shorter than Dad but well-built and attractive. Yes, she thought, Dad would approve.

"What do you think of the two of them?" she asked Stan.

"I think he is a good man, with a great head for business who can take care of himself and your mother. Now let's see if we can keep up with them." He stood, reached for Jen's hand, and they joined them on the dance floor.

Meredith tried not to hold Paul too tightly and could sense he was doing the same. "Sheer hell isn't it," he whispered in her ear.

"Yes, but we must look casual; let them get used to seeing us together. After all, I know most of the faces in the room and heaven forbid, we embarrass Jennifer."

"What will we do about tonight?" Paul asked.

"You will go to the Hyatt, and I'll meet you for breakfast, a very early breakfast," she added as she gripped his arm.

"How can I sleep knowing you are down the street?"

"Oh, I am sure you will find a way," she replied. "When do you leave again?" she asked hoping it was not tomorrow.

"Late tomorrow night, but if you can be without a car, I will fly you back to San Diego. You can have Jennifer and Stan drive the car over for you in a few days. I will suggest the idea to them myself if you would like; they might be more agreeable to saying yes. Just think, that gives us another afternoon in our friendly skies."

"It's a very short flight," Meredith replied with a smile.

"Not the route Jake flies," Paul responded with a wink, and they both laughed.

They finished a few more dances and around nine rose to leave for the Barrington home. "Time we seniors get to bed. It's been a busy day," Meredith announced.

As they walked through the country club's lobby, Jennifer asked Paul where he was staying.

"I have arranged for a room at the Hyatt, here in Indian Wells."

"You are welcome to stay in our other guest suite," she replied.

Paul smiled and said, "Thanks, maybe another time."

As Stan and Jennifer drove off in the golf cart to return home, Jen commented to Stan she thought her mother was in lust.

"How could that be?" Stan replied. "She has only known him a few weeks."

"Well, they look like quite a pair, much like you and I did when we first met."

"You might be right," Stan replied. "And I think we need to follow their direction. Let's go home and try out our master suite a bit tonight. What do you say?" She squeezed his leg in agreement and smiled.

When the attendant brought up the car Stan had provided, Paul helped Meredith into the front seat and walked to take his place behind the wheel. She realized it was the first time she had seen him drive.

"Guess you know how to handle this machine? By the way, where's Jake?"

He smiled, "Oh, he went on ahead to check us in at the hotel after dropping me off this morning. And yes, I can handle this vehicle with my eyes closed," and she was sure he could.

Paul pulled into the driveway of the Barrington house and turned to face Meredith. "Please come with me to the hotel."

"I can't, and you know it," she replied. "But I will come for coffee in the morning. How does seven sound?"

"Not early enough, my love." She pulled away before he could lean over and kiss her.

"See you at seven. Bungalow 8. I will be the one in bed alone."

She waved him away with a smile. Good night, my love, she whispered to herself and turned to go into the house.

Meredith set her travel alarm clock for 6:30 a.m. After a quick shower, she dressed in a simple blue silk sheath. She placed the diamond necklace around her neck, gave one last check to her makeup, picked up the small bag she had packed and was out the door before anyone could say "boo."

Ten minutes later she was pulling into the manicured grounds of the Hyatt Hotel. She followed the road around to the far side of the hotel property, where she knew the suites were located. Bungalow 8 was at the end of the road, so secluded one would hardly notice it, and it overlooked a small lake. She knocked and found the door ajar.

"Come in," she heard Paul say.

He stood, and she walked over to his waiting arms.

In her sexiest voice, she said, "I hope you slept well, my love, as I am here to wear you out."

He pulled her into his arms and they walked towards the bedroom. Rose petals lightly covered the comforter.

"Where did you sleep?" she wondered.

"On the couch," he replied.

He walked behind her and unzipped her sheath. It

fell to the floor and she stood naked before him. "Pretty gutsy for sixty-three, huh?" she said with a smile in her voice. "Glad I didn't get stopped by a policeman."

"I think it's wonderful," he said as he turned her to him. He fondled her breasts, leaning to kiss first one and then the other. Her head went back asking for more.

He stepped back and pulled his shirt off over his head, then reached for the sash on his sweatpants bottoms. As they fell to the floor, she found him naked and ready for her.

"Such temptations deserve a reward," Paul whispered.

"What do you have in mind?" she said breathlessly.

"This and this." He trailed kisses down her neck as he walked her to the bed. "Experience is worth something."

Paul reached down and pulled the comforter off in one John Wayne swoop and rose petals flew everywhere in the room. They both laughed at just how silly they were acting, but they didn't care. They were in love.

Meredith reclined back on the large bed, no longer shy about her body. "I want you to touch me," she whispered.

Knowing what a big step this was for Meredith, Paul's gentle hands held her face as he looked deep into her eyes and asked, "May I touch you everywhere?"

"Please," she responded.

With her permission, his hands roamed to places

they had always longed to be. He had waited for her consent and now all of her would be his. He placed kisses down her body. As he neared her core she gasped. He couldn't help but think he was going home, where he had wanted to be, and suddenly everything was so natural.

At the touch of his tongue, Meredith gasped. She had forgotten the reeling sensation oral sex produced. Paul pulled away breathless. "I have waited so long for you," he said. When she raised her head, she saw tears in his eyes.

"I love you, Paul," was all she could say.

"Come and let me love you," he said as he bent his head to her again. This time he sucked until she could not control the explosive shock of pleasure coming from her body. He stayed with her through the orgasm and she clung to him, not wanting him to stop, enjoying every second of the wild ride.

Paul rolled on top of her and entered her with powerful force. He whispered her name as he begged her to love him. Uncontrollable tears came to her.

"Are you all right?" Paul asked.

"Yes, I forgot how emotional sex can be and I will always remember today and how you make me feel. I had forgotten how to come alive inside. You brought love back to me."

Paul held her tight in his arms and added, "My darling, this is only the beginning."

Meredith decided it was either food or more sex. But she needed a rest and was sure Paul was ready for breakfast. She found warm fuzzy robes in the hotel closet while Paul called for room service. They enjoyed their meal on the private patio and soon made love again.

After dressing for the day, they decided to take a walk around the grounds of the resort. They stood arm and arm watching two young people expend way too much energy running around the tennis courts.

"I like our activities much better," Paul whispered, "and the location is so cozy and comfortable."

"Do you think they know what they're missing?" she said with a smile as she snuggled deeper into his arms.

Once back in the bungalow, Meredith called Jennifer to check in, as she had simply left a note on the kitchen island saying she was having breakfast with Paul. After all, she was trying to keep peace in the family. When she hung up, she reminded Paul, "Don't forget you volunteered to speak to Jen about transportation back to Coronado. You can ask them to take us to the airport. Thank goodness she doesn't know just how friendly those skies are."

When Meredith arrived back at Jen and Stan's home, Jennifer thought her mother had an unusual glow, and that was reinforced when Paul got there a bit later, grinning from ear to ear. Something is up with those two seniors, she thought.

Paul was quick to take charge of the day's activities and asked Jennifer if she would mind showing off her popular stores and give him a tour of El Paseo. She happily consented, and Stan, proud of his new Mercedes-Maybach, drove them through the elegant shopping district.

As they toured, Paul mentioned his private plane

and the idea of Meredith traveling back to San Diego with him. To Meredith's amazement, they thought it was a wonderful and safe idea. Jennifer and Stan were truly impressed by Paul's genuine concern and obvious love for Meredith. Later that afternoon, the foursome enjoyed a quiet early dinner at Meredith's favorite patio restaurant on El Paseo.

When they returned to Jen's, Meredith went to her room to pack for her return trip to Coronado and she was surprised when Jennifer came in, sat on her bed, and took her by the hand.

"Paul is a wonderful man. If you are as interested in him as it appears, you have my blessing. I can't imagine Claire or Stephen would be disappointed in your choice either."

Meredith hugged her daughter. "I am so happy to have your approval, Jen. We don't know where this newfound relationship will lead us, but we both care very much for each other. We shall just have to wait and see."

Jen gave her mother a quick hug and said, "The car is ready. Let's go. We can't keep our men waiting."

The four drove to the Palm Springs Executive Terminal. As they pulled up to the RCC 737 Jennifer winked at her mom.

Jake stood at the foot of the boarding ramp. Meredith was so glad to see him she kissed him on the cheek. "Next time you will let me take you where you are going, please ma'am?"

"Thank you, Jake. I'll think about it," Meredith replied.

The four of them boarded the aircraft and for once Meredith was surprised to see her always vocal daughter quiet. They walked through the plane and Paul was proud to show off the exceptional features of his 737. When they all stood in what was the obvious master bedroom, Jennifer was quick to whisper to her mom, "Make sure these skies don't get too friendly," but Meredith felt she knew they already had.

"Take care of her for us," Jen whispered to Paul as she turned to leave. Had they met Paul under different circumstances they would never expect this quiet, unassuming man to be so humble. Jennifer was happy for her mother, but she still wanted to know more about the man who had reappeared so suddenly in her mother's life.

Once Stan and Jen deplaned, Jake engaged the switch that pulled up the stairs, secured the door, and turned to take his place in the cockpit beside his co-pilot.

Meredith and Paul sat together on the short flight back to San Diego just holding hands. The crew served Meredith's favorite champagne. She began to relax but knew Paul would be leaving her again within hours and she would most likely not know where he would be going.

Upon their arrival at the San Diego Airport, they found a town car waiting at the foot of the ramp and were quickly whisked away by Jake's capable hands.

When they arrived at The Shores, Paul insisted on going through the condo to ensure all the doors and windows were secure. He tried to act nonchalant, but

Meredith suspected he was very serious and concerned for her safety.

He carried her bags to the bedroom while Meredith opened the large patio doors and prepared a promised cup of decaf coffee. Paul found her standing at the patio railing. He put his arms around her and drew her close as they stood listening to the sounds of the jagged waves rushing toward the shore. He turned her around and as he held her asked, "May I stay the night? I don't have to leave until tomorrow morning." Her kiss was his answer.

"Paul, if all of this ends tomorrow, I will have no regrets."

"It won't, I promise, my darling. I have to leave at 6 a.m. for Germany, but we have tonight. I can sleep on the plane."

As he kissed her again, she managed to add, "I think you may have to."

After their tender lovemaking, Paul slept peacefully holding Meredith. She said a silent prayer to Alex for all he had taught her about life, and the true meaning of love, and realized she was ready to commit the rest of her life to the wonderful man holding her in his arms.

In their haste to make love, Meredith realized she had forgotten to close the drapes. Only the sheers were closed. Someone might have gotten a very good view. But she rolled over and was asleep in a few minutes, the outside world forgotten.

When the alarm rang at five-thirty. Paul rolled over to encircle Meredith in his arms. She stirred.

"I'll go make the coffee," she said, in a sleepy voice.

"No," he insisted. "Jake will arrive with Starbucks in hand, and I will have breakfast on the plane."

"Oh yes, I forgot the boss has privileges."

"Yes, he does, and I am taking advantage of one right now."

"Haven't you had enough for one night?" she laughed.

"Never, and besides, it's morning," was his reply, as his hand ran up her sheer nightgown to catch one full breast.

"You want more?" she asked, as she twisted out of his grasp, and rolled over on top of him.

"More, please, more."

"Mornings are for quickies," she added, and they both laughed, as he pulled her back under him and reached for the sheet to cover them and encase them in a cocoon.

Paul knew his time was short and forced himself to release her after a brief sexual encounter, then rose for a quick shower. Meredith watched as he toweled off, refusing to leave their bed.

"I will always appreciate how you make me feel. I do love you, Paul."

"When I return, I would like to ask your children for your hand in marriage."

"You want to marry a loose senior citizen?" she said with a smile in her voice.

"I want to marry you if you will have me." She rushed to him and his arms encircled her. At that moment she knew they would be together forever.

As Meredith sensed it was time for him to leave, the tears came and Paul held her against him until he felt her calm a bit. He wanted this woman for the rest of his life.

"You must go. Jake will be waiting," and as if on cue, his cell phone rang. Jake was in the lobby.

Meredith walked to the mirror, brushed her hair, and reached for a long robe to cover her flimsy nightgown. She knew it was once again time to say goodbye. She tried to act nonchalant but found herself crying again. "I don't want you to go," she could hear herself saying, but couldn't stop the words. She had promised herself she would not plead with him.

"I don't want to leave," he said and kissed her so hard she knew their goodbye was as difficult for him as it was for her. They held each other and her lips opened. His tongue mingled with her tears. Meredith knew this man loved her with every fiber of his being.

"I'll walk you to the elevator," she said as she reached for a handful of Kleenex and linked her arm in his. As they walked down the long hall neither said a word. When the elevator came, they entered and again fell into each other's arms.

"We have to stop meeting like this," she said.

"Or buy stock in an elevator company," Paul added. When the elevator opened there stood Jake with a cup of Starbucks.

"Good morning, Mrs. Meredith," he said, smiling at Meredith. The smile she returned was a bit forlorn.

"Have a nice trip you two. Call when you find the time." She tried to keep her voice steady.

"You call Mrs. Parker if you have any problems. She always knows how to reach me."

"Thank you, my love," she answered and noticed the twinkle in Jake's eye as she uttered her words.

After waving goodbye, Meredith rode the elevator upstairs feeling almost as sad as the day she lost Alex. What if she lost Paul too?

As the black sedan left the circular driveway, a large figure peered through the drapes covering the sliding glass door of unit 708 across from Meredith's tower.

Jeffery Sanders had been planning Meredith's murder for months, spying on her through a telescope pointed at her patio. When he saw her re-enter the condo by herself, he said out loud, "She's finally alone."

Angry with himself because he had failed to kill her on the mountain, he said with hate in his voice, "I will kill you yet, old woman. You and your family will pay for all you did to me. You don't deserve to be happy, and neither does that bitch of a daughter of yours. I will see to it your new boyfriend is also eliminated. No one will stand between my getting even with your family. I won't fail again."

Meredith didn't bother with coffee but instead went back to bed sleeping on Paul's side. As she pulled the covers tight around her shoulders and smelled his distinctive cologne, she closed her eyes and was soon fast asleep.

A few hours later she was jarred awake by the ringing of the telephone. When she looked at the clock it was almost noon. She picked up the receiver and it was Jennifer, almost too cheery.

Meredith tried to stay composed. She certainly

wasn't going to tell Jen that Paul had just left her bed a few hours ago. She listened to Jen rave about Paul and how happy she was for her mother finding such a wonderful man. Meredith agreed and told her he had gone to Europe on business and would return by the end of the following week, although in truth she was not sure when he would be coming back.

She hung up the phone, crawled back under the covers, and with a smile and in the words of Rodgers and Hammerstam sang out loud, "I am in love with a wonderful guy."

CHAPTER 17

Meredith spent the rest of the day in quiet torment. Where was Paul and why all the mystery trips? She needed to know more about the man she had committed to love.

The afternoon was warm for October and she decided to enjoy a glass of wine on her patio. The sun relaxed her, and she was soon asleep. Strangely, her mind wandered back to her early childhood.

Her life began in Indiana, one in a family of four. When her mother became ill with serious asthma, the doctor advised the small family to move to a drier climate, and her parents chose to trek west. They were pleased they did not have to endure the hardships of a wagon train, but the small family felt like pioneers as they traveled in a 1948 Ford to the small southwest town of Phoenix, Arizona.

They lived in a two-bedroom house with no air conditioning, and Meredith shared a bedroom with her brother, Clark. She would always remember the one bathroom shared by the family of four.

Her father worked two jobs to make ends meet and it seemed he was never home except for dinner, as in the fifties families always ate their evening meal together. Then he was off again to his night job.

Her parents were devout Catholics and Mass was a must-attend event for all family members, one not accepted willingly by young Clark. In their early years in Phoenix, their family trips were limited to trips around the beads, a Rosary for all of you non-Catholics, but in a quiet house, in a quiet town, life went on, simple and uncomplicated.

When she was nine her parents told her she had been adopted. She was a *chosen child* as she told her younger brother who was *chosen* six years later.

Following the death of her mother when Meredith was forty-five Clark found out the details of her adoption and couldn't wait to tell his sister who her real mother was. Learning her birth mother was her father's younger sister, Cynthia Riordan, had been a shock. It turned out Meredith wasn't as special as she always believed. She was a recycled family member who had been given to her adoptive parents to raise.

Of course, she knew her Aunt Cynthia from family gatherings and stories her father told of his sister. She had been married several times and during one of those marriages had another daughter who she worshiped. Cynthia died an alcoholic at the age of seventy-five in a nursing home, abandoned by the daughter she adored, while never acknowledging her first-born child, Meredith.

When Meredith was high school age, and at an additional expense to her parents, she was enrolled at St Margaret's Girl's Academy, a private Catholic girls' school. However, Clark, a restless soul, pushed for public high school, and from the first day ran with the wrong crowd. He was the type of child that needed guidance and attention, and no one was ever there for him.

St. Margaret's was a typically strict Catholic school. In addition to standard high school subjects such as biology, geometry, and English, the girls were also required to attend daily Mass and were never allowed to smoke or drink.

Being shy and rather plain, Meredith was not one of the popular girls and her parents did not allow her to date until her final year of high school. She smiled, remembering she didn't have a date for St. Margaret's senior prom until a good friend from the local Catholic boy's school suggested they go together just so Meredith could show up.

Prom night came, and her parents' next-door neighbor, Mrs. Kennedy, seeing the lovely dress on the flat chest of the young high school senior, took her into the bedroom and promptly stuffed the top of Meredith's dress with Kleenex. "Your breasts will come," her mother's friend promised her, "but not in time for tonight's prom."

That night when she returned home from the dance Meredith prayed for large breasts.

Once in college, her breasts did grow and so did her shapely legs. Meredith was becoming attractive and all of a sudden boys noticed her.

Not many students had cars and her father allowed her the use of the family vehicle only one day a week since gas was twenty-five cents a gallon. She would take a few of her girlfriends and they would cruise around the local Bob's Big Boy Drive Inn.

During her college days, she began running with the in-crowd and even pledged a sorority. Friday nights were devoted to college football games. After one such game, while standing outside with her two friends, Jane and Karen, the star quarterback came running out of the locker room and ran straight into Meredith, almost knocking her over. He apologized, reaching for her arm to steady her, and that was all it took. Paul Richardson looked into her eyes, and fell head over heels, as the old saying goes.

She remembered how jealous her friends were when she and Paul started dating. She had accidentally snagged the handsome jock, with his dark skin, short-cropped hair, and quick running ability. He was always the one hurling the ball or himself down the field for the next touchdown. She was suddenly popular and accepted everywhere on the arm of the big man on campus.

Paul found a deserted spot on a riverbank and it became their place to make out a lot. Meredith never asked how he knew of the place but felt he probably had been there many times before.

One afternoon after the longest kiss they had ever experienced, he reached for one of her now larger breasts and Meredith heard Paul say "I love you." She instantly knew things were out of control. They didn't have classes about sex education in those days, but they were both aware of where those kinds of kisses and actions led, and by the size of the bulge in his jeans she knew they were getting into uncharted territory. Meredith admired him a great deal but knew

218

love for this boy, not yet a man was not her life's destiny.

As she carefully slid from his embrace, Paul caught her by the shoulders. He knew he had moved too fast, but the words had come straight from his heart. "Will you think about loving me back?" He had asked shyly, and all Meredith could do was nod her head and look puzzled, which was exactly how she felt.

Later that evening, joining her family on their trip around the beads Meredith prayed she would make the right decision. She didn't want to hurt Paul but felt she could never love him the way he deserved to be loved. To lead him on would be a terrible mistake.

Meredith needed to talk to someone, but in those days young women, especially young Catholic women, didn't have a counselor to talk with about issues of the heart. Even most Catholic mothers hesitated to discuss sexual relations with their daughters. This was certainly the situation for Meredith. So, she made the hard decision on her own to end her relationship with Paul.

Meredith smiled as she remembered her promise to herself to wait for Mr. Right, but would he ever come her way? She would save herself for him just in case. *No meant no* and boys didn't argue. Oh, life was simple in the glory days of the fifties.

As she lay on the lounge chair looking out at the beautiful Pacific Ocean, she wondered about her inner struggles with Paul. What if she had said yes then? Where would they both be today? He had admitted to her their lost love was the motivation for his lifelong career. Now after all these years they had found each other again.

A cool dash of ocean air made her stir, but soon she was back to her daydreaming, lost in her past.

During her second year of college, her parents had allowed her to move into an apartment a couple of blocks from campus with two of her sorority sisters. It was small with only basic furniture and a few pots and pans, but the word *roommates* had a glorious ring to it.

Dan Meyers, one of her classmates in second-year literature, approached Meredith about showing off her beautiful legs and modeling for his life-drawing class. He was an art major and she would always treasure the memory of all those faces staring at her. They sketched her body, each with their own unique vision. She was the center of attention and it was the biggest confidence builder in her life.

Jane kidded her about posing nude for the next year's class. "There will be no nudity until Mr. Right comes along," Meredith was quick to respond. Not so with Jane, who Meredith knew was spending nights at the home of her fraternity boyfriend.

She chanced a few dates with a certain bad boy in town after they shared a cherry coke at a local drive-in. Being seen with Eric Deller boosted her popularity, but she soon realized she wasn't sure in which direction.

For a few dates, nothing passed between them except kisses, and not very good ones, if her older mind was remembering clearly. Her roommate, Jane, questioned her daily about the wild sex she knew had to be going on in the back seat of Eric's car, but Meredith reassured her nothing had happened.

One evening she and Eric went up to their favorite mountain top to park. After a few hot moments, he reached for her hand. She realized he had unzipped his jeans and he placed her hand in his pants. She had never felt anything like that before. Oh, she had read about it in her textbooks, seen photos describing what a man looked like when aroused, but never felt anything so warm and yet hard at the same time. She was startled by its size. Meredith tried to pull her hand away, but he kept it pinned in place. He began moving against her palm.

Meredith panicked. Sex was for lovemaking and she certainly didn't love Eric Deller. With her free hand, she reached to the right and felt her small handbag. In one swift move, she snatched the purse and swung it as hard as she could, hitting Eric across the left eye. He gasped, and dropped Meredith's hand, reaching instead for his eye. He was bleeding and suddenly a new passion developed—*anger*.

Meredith was terrified. She moved to the door and flung it open. She could run, but where? She stopped a few feet from the car, crying so hard she was shaking and froze as he exited the car. Eric stood buttoning his jeans, staring at her. How was he going to react?

To her surprise, as he walked closer, he said, "I'm sorry, Meredith. It is my usual date routine and I guess you aren't ready yet. Come on kid, I will take you back to your place." He held the car door open for her like a perfect gentleman. Meredith got into the car and they drove in silence back to her apartment.

Meredith was reluctant to discuss the evening's events with her two roommates, but the next morning as they shared breakfast, she told them what had happened. They agreed that with the school semester almost over, it was time to give up their meager apartment. All three decided to return to the security of their families and she knew she would never date Eric Deller again.

Meredith continued joining the family in their nightly trip around the beads, but it was summer vacation, she was nineteen years old and needed something to do outside of the house. She wanted a job.

She answered an ad in the Phoenix Examiner newspaper for a counter clerk at the cosmetic counter of a Walgreens Drug store and was interviewed by an overly made-up redheaded woman in her mid-fifties who saw Meredith as a dutiful, simple employee who would do whatever she was told.

Meredith saw something different. She saw an opportunity to learn how to apply makeup, sell, and meet people. She began work the following week. She stocked and cleaned shelves, moved merchandise, and waited on customers, her favorite part of the job.

Her personality came alive in that small Walgreens Drug Store in a downtown Phoenix mall. A new Meredith was emerging. Without knowing it, she was setting herself on a course for success. Little did she know that twenty-five years later she would be a successful entrepreneur dusting her own shelves.

The second semester of her sophomore year at college was coming to a close. Her grades were above average and she loved her part-time job. Then one day her father came home with a special request of his daughter. Would she please go out with the son of his executive secretary, Helen?

The young man had just come home from a tour of duty with the Navy in Japan. He was stationed in San Diego and was coming to Phoenix for a long weekend to visit his family. "It's just one afternoon out of your busy life," her father had said. How could she refuse?

She went as a favor to her father. It was the first date of the rest of her life.

CHAPTER 18

A cool breeze stirred Meredith from her reminiscences. She was surprised when she realized she had been daydreaming for most of the afternoon. She must have dozed off, something she seldom did, but after her frightening trip and busy weekend of lovemaking with Paul she must have been more tired than she realized.

She felt strange reliving so many forgotten memories. She had been so fortunate to meet Alex on that blind date. She would never forget their years together, and still struggled internally whether she had the right to set them aside for this new relationship with Paul.

Nothing seemed simple but, for now, she needed to get inside, close up the condo and prepare dinner for one. She tried to watch television, even picked up the same book she had taken to Hawaii and DC, but still couldn't concentrate. Questions about Paul seemed to be her only focus lately.

Three days passed, or was it four? Meredith's car was still at Jennifer's since Paul had flown her home. She was surprised at the inconvenience of not having a car readily available so she was pleased when Jen called and told her Stan had a business meeting to attend in San Diego. He planned to drop the car off at

Meredith's condo the next morning and take a cab to his meeting.

Paul had not called and the longer she waited, the more nervous she became about his constant disappearances. When the phone rang around eight that evening, she answered hoping it was Paul but surprised to hear her son Stephen on the line.

"Hi, Mom, how's it going?" was always the way he started his calls.

"Oh, Stephen. It's so good to hear from you. How are Loren and the children?"

"Doing well, thanks, and still loving their British lifestyle. I may never get them back to the US. Speaking of the States, what are you doing this weekend? Any chance there is an empty bed for me in Coronado?"

Meredith's heart leaped. "Of course," she replied. "I can't believe you are coming to San Diego."

"I have government business in DC on Monday. And since I have a few days of annual leave time I should take, I can route myself to hang out with my favorite mom if she is available."

"Stephen, you don't know how much I want to see you. Things are happening in my life, and I need to talk to you."

Concerned, Stephen inquired, "Are you feeling okay?"

"Oh yes, I am fine." But she wanted to add my heart is a mess and not the way you might expect. "When do you arrive?"

"On Thursday and I have three nights I can be in San Diego."

"I will be at the airport to pick you up at the usual

spot. Just send me your airline, flight number, and arrival time." Stephen's unexpected visit was the best news she could receive and a way to tell him about the new man in her life.

"Thanks, Mom. I am looking forward to seeing you. My flight is from London on British Airways and after a quick change of planes, I'll be on the way to you around 4 p.m. I will call you from Los Angeles," and after a quick goodbye, he was off the line.

As she hung up the phone she couldn't help but think of the wonderful visit she had experienced in England with Stephen, Loren, and their twins Samantha and Derrick. It was a few short months after Alex had died so suddenly and had been her first long-distance trip alone. She realized it was time to see more of her grandchildren before they grew up and moved on with their lives.

Meredith had now gone four days without hearing from the man who professed to love her. She dismissed the first two days as travel and busy European meetings, but couldn't he at least find time to call? After all, cell phones are everywhere these days.

A couple of hours later the phone rang. She picked up the receiver and prayed.

"Hello, Sunshine."

"Oh, Paul what is going on? I was getting so worried. Where are you? How are you?" The questions came too fast she realized, but she was both excited and upset.

"Sorry, I have been in a remote area of the

world," not offering to tell her where. "I just wasn't able to call. Sometimes my life isn't my own, and I hope you believe me when I say things will change. I am winding up several large projects before I head to DC, then on to be with my favorite girl. I want to be home with you every night. I have the perfect hideaway chosen for our retirement, I promise you, my love."

What could she say? He was confessing his love, and Meredith wanted so much to believe him.

She changed the subject by telling him of her recent phone call from Stephen, but he already knew her son was coming for a visit. That only made him realize even more how much he needed to come clean about his life of secrets.

"He will be in DC next week. Maybe you two can arrange to meet."

How could they not meet, Paul thought? He will be in my office for an interview. He may be joining my team at the State Department.

What will she think when she finally finds out the truth about what I do for a living?

"I would love to meet your son. Have him call Mrs. Parker," he said casually, not knowing what else to say.

They talked for at least an hour when it seemed Paul was forced to break off the conversation. "I must go, my darling, but I will try and call you in a few days. Don't worry if you don't hear from me. I will be back in touch with you as soon as I can. You can always call Mrs. Parker. She can find me in case of an emergency."

After quick *I love you's* the line went dead and

Meredith sat alone, wondering why Mrs. Parker could always reach Paul, but she couldn't.

Oh well, she had Stephen on his way to visit and would concentrate on him for the next few days. She would have to take Paul at his word. "But, how can I go on waiting for phone calls from faraway places and wishing Paul home?" she said out loud. "This is not the way I want to live my life."

Meredith spent the next few days getting ready for her son's visit. She was so excited she hardly had time to miss Paul, but of course, she did, every moment. She cooked some of Stephen's favorite dishes and had a box of chocolate Junior Mints to tuck under his pillow just like she did when he was a child. He would laugh and make fun of her, but she knew he wouldn't mind. Having her son to herself didn't happen often and Meredith wanted to ask him to help her find out more about Paul by using his government contacts.

Stephen called from the Los Angeles Airport once his international flight had landed. Meredith monitored his arrival time and was over the bridge and at the San Diego Airport in her best average time of twelve minutes.

He looked as handsome as ever and her eyes filled with tears at the sight of him. She pulled to the curb and scooted over to the passenger side. Stephen jumped in and took the wheel. With an awkward hug across the wide seat, Meredith said, "I have missed you so much." Soon they were re-crossing the large expanse of the Coronado Bridge, a task he had done many times since his college days.

Stephen settled in the guest room while Meredith set the dinner table out on the patio. The weather was perfect, and he thanked her for preparing his favorite spaghetti pie, and they laughed and talked for hours.

Around eight the phone rang and to her surprise it was Paul. Meredith told him Stephen had arrived. "Enjoy your son, my love and I will try to call you tomorrow," and of course added, "I love you, more than life itself."

She whispered, "I love you too," and was quick to return to the patio to watch the beautiful ocean sunset with Stephen.

But Paul's words played around in her head. *More than life itself.* What had he meant? Was he in some sort of danger?

With the time change and long airplane flight, Meredith knew Stephen would be tired and by nine, his usual bedtime, he trotted off to bed. She did a quick clean-up of the kitchen, preparing her usual coffee for the morning and setting out a teacup for Stephen. That child never had learned to drink coffee.

It was very special to wake up, walk into the kitchen and find Stephen sitting cross-legged reading the newspaper. It was his morning ritual. The sight of him almost brought her to tears.

Stephen had been her main source of support when Alex died, but their visits always included his family, never just mother and son alone. Meredith walked up to his broad shoulders and kissed the top of his balding head. Guess working for the government causes baldness, she had always teased him.

"Did you sleep well, Stephen?" she asked.

"Great, Mom, thanks. Nothing like fresh beach air to make you sleep like a log."

"How about a walk down the beach with your mom?"

They walked arm in arm down the beach walk. Nearing the Hotel del Coronado, they headed across the sand toward the water. Stephen seemed so quiet, and Meredith knew there was something on his mind.

Walking back, they found a bench, sat down to rest and he took her hand. Her mother's instinct took over and knew something was wrong.

"Mom, I may be relocating to the States."

"Oh, Stephen, I would love to have you closer. Is a wonderful transfer in order?"

"Yes, but if I return, I may be returning alone."

Meredith stared at him in surprise. "What do you mean?"

"Loren and the children may not be moving with me. They want to stay in England. They love their lifestyle in Leeds. Things have not gone well for Loren and me this past year, and although we still love each other very much, we feel time apart would do us both good. It would give each of us some breathing room."

"Breathing room, what do you mean? Are you considering divorce?"

"No, not yet, but we need time apart to weigh our life over the past year. This has been a year of numerous international crises, and Loren and I have become distant. There is so much about my professional life I am not allowed to discuss with her. You and dad could discuss anything. I can't come home and talk to Loren about any of the events that happen during my day. A secret life is just that—secret. And Derrick and Samantha are so involved in their British surroundings, they won't miss me."

Stephen took a breath and Meredith's heart ached for him. All she could think of was Paul. There were so many secrets revolving around him. Would their life together be like Stephen's? Was love ever enough?

She reached for Stephen's hand to comfort him. What to say and how to respond to his news took her a moment. She knew how difficult it was to come to her and confess his family situation. In today's modern world divorce came all too easily as she had already found out. Two daughters divorced and now her only son considering leaving his family and moving far away from them for his career.

"I won't judge you, Stephen. You are a grown man and must make your own decisions. I can only hope your time apart will help you and Loren come to the best conclusion for your family."

"Thanks, Mom. I was hoping you would understand and not be critical. You are the only proper woman on the planet. I love you and need your support."

"Of course, you have my support, Stephen, but there is something else we need to talk about. Your mother is not as proper as you may think."

"Oh, Mom, don't even go there. You and dad shared a perfect marriage."

"Stephen, no one is perfect." Meredith felt it was her turn to tell her son about the affair she was having with a certain gentleman from Washington, DC, but didn't know how to begin. She still needed time to think.

"Let's head back to the condo and have an early dinner on the patio while the sun is still warm."

They rose and walked in silence, Meredith now understanding why Stephen seemed so sad. She reached for his hand and he took hers without hesitation knowing he had someone to trust.

What will he think when I tell him of the events of the past few weeks? And what will I tell him of my love for a man other than his father?

Stephen had been recruited by the government as a field agent while still in college, and after graduation, he and his wife Loren relocated to Washington, DC. While stationed in DC, they welcomed twins Derrick and Samantha.

Luckily for the winter-loving family, their next assignment had been to the Colorado Rockies. His office was near Cheyenne Mountain where many secret events transpired underground. Since Colorado, they had lived in multiple exotic places around the world. They were currently living in Leeds a few hours from London, definitely not exotic, but so far one of their favorites.

The twins, now thirteen, spoke with delightful British accents and after four years living in the UK, were exceptional tour guides. Meredith had visited them twice since Alex's death and had been awed by everything they knew of the beautiful English countryside with its wonderful old castles and quaint cottages. They had taken the fast train to London,

233

spent fun days shopping, and even attended a matinee of *Mama Mia*, one of the wonderful plays showing in the West End.

The family loved their European lifestyle, school, and their many British friends, and were happy and content, or so it seemed to Meredith. However, as much as Stephen enjoyed his work and living all over the world, it appeared maintaining the required level of secrecy was not easy and was leading to undue stress between he and Loren.

Mother and son spent Saturday quietly, lounging around her condo and walking on the beach again. Stephen enjoyed the Navy fliers' touch-and-goes as much as Alex had, and his eyes turned skywards each time the planes came out for maneuvers.

Stephen showed off the pictures he had brought of the kids and told her of the various trips and excursions they had taken as a family.

Meredith drank in the stories, asking him many questions as she basked in their one-on-one time together. But always in the back of her mind was the need to muster the courage to tell her son about Paul and their recently rekindled romance. As hard as she tried, the time never seemed quite right to broach the subject.

Early Sunday morning Stephen was busy packing his suitcase preparing for his flight to DC. He had big meetings ahead and he suspected a major decision to make that would affect the rest of his career. He knew it would be a long and complicated tour of duty. His interview was at State Department headquarters and depending on the offer, he was prepared to move back to Washington, and take the job. He was one-of-a-kind, both in knowledge and status, and his superiors had tapped him for the interview. They needed him and if the offer was what he was expecting, he would not refuse.

The smell of Mom's coffee drew him to the kitchen. There was Mother Meredith as he sometimes called her in one of her Loretta Young floral gowns and matching peignoir. She had made his favorite tea and held his cereal bowl in her hand.

He knew it was hard for her to smile under the circumstances, but she had kept her promise and not been judgmental. He had things to work through and she was determined not to stand in his way. But time was slipping away for her to tell Stephen about her affair with Paul, so she took a deep breath and began. "Son, I need to talk to you. I have met someone and become very fond of him."

"You what, Mom?"

"Yes, Stephen, you heard me, I have a new gentleman friend. Jennifer has met him and likes him very much."

"Mom, are you serious? No, Mom, are you serious?"

Meredith took a deep breath. "Yes, I think it is very serious, as serious as two seniors can be."

"Do you want to marry him?"

"I might," Meredith replied.

"And here I am feeling guilty telling you of my plans. You seem to be making a few plans of your own," Stephen replied.

"No plans as of yet, Stephen. The gentleman is an old friend from my college days. We met on my recent trip to Washington, DC. We knew each other many years ago in Phoenix. His wife is deceased and he has two sons near your age who work in his business."

"Well, well, Mom, you surprise me. How far has this little chance meeting taken you?"

"You said I was the last of the proper women on earth. Well, I don't think I have been acting very proper, but at my age, life's short. Your father and I had discussed what would happen for the surviving spouse as we grew older, and both agreed we wanted the other to be happy. And I am very happy."

"Well, mom, I'm surprised—not shocked, but surprised. You are a very attractive woman and a fine catch for any man. What's this man's name and what does he do?"

"His name is Paul Richardson and he is in the construction business," Meredith calmly replied, shaking his cereal into a bowl.

Startled, Stephen froze in place trying not to act shocked as he clasped his hands together to gain control of himself. How had his mother managed to fall for one of the top covert agents assigned to the State Department?

"How did you meet this man, Mom?" Stephen managed to ask in his calmest government voice.

"You remember my trip to visit Dr. Karen. Well, she took me to a dinner party at some Washington bigwig's home. It was surprising two old friends would run into each other in that large city and at a government social function."

Not as unusual as you might think Mom, Stephen thought, as Richardson's main office is located down the block from the White House, right where he was headed for his meeting tomorrow.

"It's a long story son, how much time do you have?"

"Not much, so give me a quick overview."

Meredith quickly gave him the condensed version of their meeting, their vacation in Hawaii, and the events on the mountainside en route to Palm Springs.

Stephen was shocked to hear about her close call on the road. But the part of her story that caught him off-guard the most was the name of his mother's new beau. How in the world could she be sleeping with the man he had an appointment with at nine a.m. tomorrow morning, and a man he had worked with for over nine years. He realized she had no idea who Paul Richardson truly was.

Meredith saw the questions in his eyes but all he could reply was, "Mom, I am speechless," and he truly was. The government certainly keeps its secrets well, he thought with a smile.

"Good for you," was all that came out of his mouth and Meredith smiled. He rose and took her in his arms. "Whatever makes you happy, Mom."

She held him close and felt she was finally able to relax after her confessions. Meredith thought he accepted her news, as she had done with his.

They said their airport goodbyes in the kitchen. Within a few minutes, he had gathered his bags, snapped on his tie, and they were in the car headed for the airport. "Keep me posted on your new man," he said when she dropped him off at the airport curb.

Meredith was quick to offer him good luck with the job offer, and he was off to the plane with a wave.

When he was settled in the window seat on his United Airlines flight to Washington, Stephen struggled to try to decide just how to introduce himself to Paul. How would his being Meredith Evans' son affect the rest of his career?

Well Mom, you sure snagged a good man. He has one of the finest reputations in government. There had even been rumors the government's inner circle spoke with him about running for vice president a few years ago, but he declined the offer. He smiled, thinking of his mom as the Second Lady. She had always been the first lady in his eyes.

Stephen reminded himself to be sure to telephone Loren with his mother's news. She would also be excited and happy for Meredith. But in the next instance, Stephen wondered if she would even want to talk to him. They had been married many years but it was as if they had been living separate lives much of the time. He loved his children and deeply loved Loren, but his career always seemed to come first.

Over the years he had often wondered how his mother and father balanced their work and love life so perfectly. Compromise and honesty, he guessed, but with his line of work, there was never much of a choice. Everything was a secret.

Tomorrow would be a very unusual meeting, he thought. He needed to be mentally prepared to meet with Paul. He was sure Mr. Richardson knew his meeting was with Meredith Evans' only son. Just what did the government have in mind for him?

He smiled as he ordered a scotch and water. Mom, you will need to learn a whole new set of balancing acts to keep up with Paul Richardson. I hope you're ready for what you are letting yourself in for.

Finishing his drink, he put on the airplane headphones and was soon asleep.

CHAPTER 19

Paul was busy finalizing construction on a new government building near Damascus in the Middle East. While the project was large, complicated, and extremely dangerous, the security installation for the two hundred thousand square foot State Department main building was almost finished.

When he had a moment to think of something other than government specifications, his thoughts were of Meredith and her safety. He promised himself this would be his last job. He no longer had the desire to be in danger for the government, nor did he need the money. Meredith was now his primary focus in life.

He hoped he would only need a day in Washington to go over the details with the fellow staffers from the Department and interview the young man who would be waiting in his office lobby. When he checked his calendar, he realized how busy his schedule was. He felt desperate to find someone he trusted to take over that full calendar so he could walk away and into Meredith's arms.

He had been thinking about his sons in recent days and wanted to become a more important part of their lives. More than anything he wanted to meld his family and Meredith's together. He decided he would see the boys as soon as he returned to the States and arrange for them to meet *his Meredith*, as he now called her. He felt certain they would accept her as the mother they had missed for these past years. He wanted to retire and be able to explain what he could of his past. He hoped they would all understand his covert lifestyle and respect his patriotism.

Meredith was unaware Paul was having her guarded 24-hours a day after the incident on the mountain. He had received word of a suspicious man on the grounds of the El Cortez tower, but reportedly the man was a gardener. Paul was pleased to know Stephen was visiting for the next three days and was excited he would soon be there to take over her protection himself.

He couldn't dismiss the thought he might be responsible for making Meredith a target. He had made many enemies in his years spent in international espionage for the government, and someone who knew of his love for Meredith might try to hurt him by targeting her.

His executive suite at the Four Seasons in Damascus was large and very lonely. It was located on Shukri Al Quatli Street in the center of the city. Most evenings he ate alone and went to bed early, dreaming Meredith was beside him. Calls were difficult and could be traced, so telephone usage was limited, and not being able to talk with her made him miss her even more. He wanted to go home and convince her to marry him.

He would be on his way to DC in two days and

they would definitely talk marriage. But how much could he share with her? Could he tell her that for the past twenty-plus years he had used his construction company as a cover for the dangerous work he had done for the State Department in foreign countries? His signed agreement with the department stated he was not to divulge his secret assignments to anyone, not even his family, and except for Jake, he had honored that agreement.

Before Meredith, the danger never mattered and the secrecy did not seem so constricting, but now he was anxious to give up the excitement of international intrigue for an evening at home with the woman he loved.

Paul and his aide left early the next morning for the project site, very aware of the problems posed by traveling along the outer roads of Damascus. His bulletproof Suburban purred down the highway sandwiched in the middle of a caravan of vehicles when suddenly an explosion ripped through the air behind them and he watched in horror as the trailing truck lifted straight into the air from what had to be the power of an IED.

Paul and his driver pulled to the side of the road, both shaken. That was the closest he had been to danger in a long time, and it was going to be the last if he had anything to say about it. They jumped from the car to help the two men trapped inside the wreckage. As they pulled the bodies from the burning car, he tried to calm himself. He knelt beside them, saw the blood, and knew the two men were dead. A shudder went through his body. It could have easily been him and, suddenly Catholic again, made a quick sign of the cross.

To maintain his cover, Paul knew he could not be identified at a crime scene. He needed to get away from the area as soon as possible. He contacted his office, filed a report, and was forced to leave the bodies beside the road.

Within hours he had the right people in place and following a few quick meetings with his staffers, conducted a debriefing, and headed to the airport for his flight to Washington. As he boarded the plane, he took a deep breath, happy to be on his way home. After today's attack, he decided *no more, it's over for me*, as he took a stiff drink of scotch.

He tried to sleep, but every time he closed his eyes, he saw his two innocent co-workers lying on the roadside covered in blood. Middle Eastern warriors were a different breed. You never knew when or where they would strike. Had he been the real target?

When he finally dozed off there were no dreams. He woke almost eight hours later somewhere over the Atlantic. It was the most rest he had in succession in days.

Checking his watch, he calculated the time and knew it was the middle of the night in California. Even knowing Meredith could help calm his shattered nerves, he knew it was much too early to call, especially since he was not able to explain why he was so shaken. He needed to get hold of himself before he faced her to confess as much as he was able about his top-secret career.

CHAPTER 20

Jeffery Sanders had been making plans to destroy the Evans family since Jennifer's attorney told him he would no longer receive any more money. Figuring the best way to hurt her was through her beloved parents, he began his plan of destruction. Alex's sudden death saved Jeffery one step in his revenge. Now it was time to take care of the missus. He wanted to hurt her. No, he wanted her dead.

He had begun watching her over a year ago. Jeff had tracked Meredith down through a mutual friend, who had no idea of his true motives. He was sure Meredith never knew she was being watched. He sat on the sea wall as she passed by, was in the next aisle in the grocery store, and even parked near her at her favorite bakery. With dark glasses, a hat pulled down low, and his face hidden behind a beard and mustache, she never noticed him.

Between odd jobs and the drugs he pushed, he finally had enough money to rent a small studio unit across from Meredith at The Shores. He could easily sneak into the parking garage of her building using his guest pass, but for his plan to work he needed the parking spot next to hers to be empty.

He had been monitoring the garage and presumed the unit assigned to that space was not rented as it had been sitting vacant for over two months. He planned to park there and when she entered the garage, grab Meredith from behind, put the rag of chloroform over her face, and shove her into the front seat of his car. That empty parking space was all he needed. Well, that and some luck to determine when she would be in the garage.

Fortunately for him, using his telescope he could see through to Meredith's front door. As long as he stayed vigilant, in the time it took her to go down the elevator and walk to the garage, he could drive to the empty parking space next to her car in time to abduct her.

Jeff calculated the drive out to Yuma at almost three hours and he would see she didn't wake up during the trip. Once in the desert, he would kill her and bury the body where no one would ever find it. Revenge was a strong motive and the cocaine he sniffed helped. Jeffery Sanders was ready to put his murderous plan into action.

He had seen Stephen leave and the new man in her life had not been around in days, so he knew Meredith was alone again. Not wanting to be spaced out, he still needed to fortify his courage with a small sniff of coke. This was the big day. He didn't want another screw-up like the one that happened on the mountain road.

When he saw Meredith close her patio door and walk toward the front door, he quickly got in his car and drove to her building, using his remote gate access to enter her underground parking garage. He parked in the open space next to Meredith's driver's side door and pretended to be cleaning out his car while he waited for her. He was wearing a uniform taken from one of The Shores' maintenance sheds and looked very official. Although the garage was monitored by surveillance cameras, Jeffery felt well-hidden between the cars.

A bit nervous, he had only a few minutes to wait until the building's lobby garage door opened and Meredith walked towards her car, not noticing her surroundings as usual. She was probably on the way into town to run errands or have her hair done, he thought snidely.

Just as she reached for the handle of her car door, Jeffery snaked his arm around her and covered her nose and mouth with a chloroform-soaked rag. She struggled briefly and then suddenly collapsed against the door as the sweet-smelling sedative took over.

Jeffery quickly pulled her into the front seat of his car and clicked the seat belt around her, not wanting to take any chances at being stopped by the cops. He threw her purse in the back seat of her car and pushed the automatic door locks. By the time anyone discovered Meredith was missing and searched her car, the old woman would be dead.

Be calm Jeff, he almost said out loud. He walked around, seated himself in the driver's seat, and started the engine. He drove carefully out of the underground garage, not wanting to draw attention to himself. He glanced over to check his hostage and found Meredith still sleeping soundly, her head resting back on the seat. They were over the bridge and on the freeway en route to the desert city of Yuma before Jeff had a chance to look at her again.

He thought he heard her moan. Fearful of her

wakening, he decided it was time to move her to the trunk. He came to the roadside turn he had marked on Interstate 8 and pulled off the freeway onto a side road. With no cars in view, he picked up her lifeless body, put the rag to her nose again, and placed her in the trunk. He was sure she would stay unconscious for the rest of the drive.

Meredith was confused as she slowly woke and tried to move in the very confined space. Instant panic set in. Where was she and who was she with? She lay still trying to calm herself. It didn't help. She could feel tears rolling down her cheeks and realized she was not tied up but felt drowsy and couldn't focus. She had a slight headache and there was an overly sweet odor on her hands she didn't recognize.

Reaching for her handbag, she realized it was no longer on her arm and suddenly registered she was in the trunk of a car and whoever put her there had taken the purse.

What did he want? Money? Would he try and rape her?

When she rolled her head to the side, she hit something cold and sharp. She realized it was a shovel by the long handle that ran the length of her body. Was this person planning to dig her grave? Did someone want her dead?

Meredith tried to roll over to get away from the cold metal head of the shovel and felt something hard against her hip.

"Oh, my cell phone is in my pants pocket and he didn't find it," she whispered to herself. She quickly opened it and was blinded by the light it produced. A message from Jen popped up but Meredith ignored it and paged down to Paul's private line. Mrs. Parker answered in one ring.

"Help me, Mrs. Parker," Meredith whispered in a panicked voice. She quickly relayed what little she knew and in between sobs begged, "Find Paul and find me. Please hurry."

Mrs. Parker tried to calm her but unfortunately had to put Meredith on hold as she dialed the appropriate State Department and San Diego Sheriff's offices. When a businessman working covertly for the US Government reaches out in distress, all local agencies jump to respond.

At the same time, she was deciding how best to break this news to her superior somewhere in the skies over the North Atlantic if she calculated correctly. This would surely panic him, as she knew how much he loved this woman.

Mrs. Parker quickly came back on the line to Meredith and guaranteed help was on the way. She then talked a panicked Meredith through the steps to ensure the GPS on her phone was turned on so the local and state police could track her location. Mrs. Parker knew telling Meredith she was being followed by the authorities would help calm her nerves.

Once she had all agencies working on Meredith's abduction, Margaret Parker felt it was time to make the call she dreaded the most, to her supervisor.

Paul was seated, organizing his paperwork for his upcoming meetings. He would be landing in DC within the hour and he was so intent on the report he was startled when his private phone line rang. He

249

answered with his usual, "Yes, Mrs. Parker."

"You better sit down, sir, and get hold of yourself."

"Another crisis?" he asked.

"Yes, and you are going to go ballistic over what I have to tell you," she replied.

"What now?" Paul responded with a sigh.

"I have Meredith on the other line. I have no way to tell you but to blurt it out. Sir, she has been kidnapped and is in the trunk of a car headed somewhere down the 8 Freeway out of San Diego."

Paul shot out of his seat and began shouting at her. "What in God's name is going on?"

"Calm yourself, sir," came the response from an always calm Mrs. Parker.

"How can I calm myself? Where is Meredith?"

"We don't know, sir," she responded.

"What do you mean, you don't know? Who got the message to you?"

"She did."

"What are you saying, Mrs. Parker?" he shouted into the phone.

"The abductor took her handbag, but she happened to have her cell phone in her pocket. When she woke in the trunk, untied, she rolled over and felt the phone."

Mrs. Parker continued with every detail of her conversation with Meredith. She told him of working with Meredith to turn on her phone's GPS and the police action being taken in cooperation with the San Diego Sheriff's office.

"How in the hell could anyone get to her? I am having her watched."

"Obviously not close enough, Sir," she responded dryly, and she politely told him again to calm down.

"Sir, stop talking and listen. I am going to patch you through. Do not say a word, let me do the talking." Reluctantly, Paul did as he was told. Mrs. Parker was a trained agent and had specialized in hostage situations for years.

Paul stood frozen to the spot with a stranglehold on his phone. He had to strain to hear, as he knew several other phones were also listening on the line. He could hear Meredith breathing.

"Roll over Meredith," Mrs. Parker told her. "Pretend you are still drugged."

"Mrs. Parker, the car is stopping. What shall I do?" she said with panic in her voice.

"How much cell phone battery is left?" Mrs. Parker asked.

Meredith glanced and said in a shaky voice, "Two bars."

"Leave the phone on so the police can continue to track you. Put it back in your pocket," she ordered. "We will monitor your conversation."

Meredith did as she was told. Crying, she begged her to find Paul, her son, or someone to help her, and then pretended to sleep as Mrs. Parker had ordered.

Paul could hear the trunk lid open and a man's voice said coldly, "Well, little lady, looks like you are still asleep. We don't have far to go now." He then heard the trunk lid close.

Once again in the dark Meredith reached for her cell phone. "Did you hear him, Mrs. Parker?"

"Yes, dear, try and stay calm. Help is on the way."

For once Paul did as he was told, which didn't happen often, and did not acknowledge he was on the line. The situation was out of his hands and he knew it.

"Have you contacted Paul?" Meredith sobbed. Hearing that, his heart ached.

"Yes, and he is somewhere in the air returning to Washington, but the local police are tracking you. How is the cell battery holding up?"

"Still two bars left. What do I do?"

"Try and remain calm. Turn the phone off until you hear the car stop. Then turn it back on but leave it in your pocket. I have units in the area tracking your every move."

Mrs. Parker had been through many such situations in her life, but helping Meredith was different. Her superior, one of the finest men she had ever known, was deeply in love with this woman. She heard the phone click off and Paul was instantly back on the line.

"Great job, Mrs. Parker. You must keep her calm. Where do we stand?"

"We have units following the car and others racing to the area. We think the driver is on the way to Arizona through Yuma. There are border police ready to stop him. Our guess is he will turn off somewhere before Yuma. He must have a plan in mind."

"My plane has been turned around and headed towards California. We will have to stop for fuel but can be back in the air within minutes. Jake has already requested permission to land at a US airbase. He has the airport on alert, fuel trucks waiting on the tarmac, and he plans to make this refueling stop quicker than an Indy race car pit stop.

"I know the San Diego sheriffs will arrive before I can get to the area. You may be right about the kidnapper trying to cross the border into Arizona and if that happens it becomes an FBI case."

Mrs. Parker took a deep breath. "Sir, we will find her and bring her back to you safe and sound."

Paul knew she had set all the right systems in place. He thanked her, but inside was trembling with fear for Meredith's life. It would take him at least four hours to get to her location. He could only pray they would find her alive. She had to be. She just had to be.

Meredith shivered in the trunk. She lay very still as Mrs. Parker had ordered. Thank God for cell phones and Mrs. Parker, she thought. She prayed Paul would find her and all of a sudden found herself making an imaginary trip around the beads, one she had not taken in many years. Someone had to save her, maybe it would be God. She had found Paul again, and her children and grandchildren needed her.

She felt the car slow and then turn to the right. Meredith switched her cell phone back on and Mrs. Parker responded in an instant.

"The car has turned off the freeway. The driver turned to the right and the road is very bumpy."

"We're with you," came Mrs. Parker's response.

"Oh my God, I am down to one bar on the cell phone. What do I do?"

"Turn it off again and only turn it on when you feel the car stopping."

"All right," she replied and was gone off the line.

Paul sat monitoring the call and could hardly stand the pressure growing in his chest. He prayed to God and hoped Meredith could somehow sense he was on his way. He wanted so much to speak to her, but she was doing better taking orders from Mrs. Parker. He knew he could not keep his emotions in check if he spoke to her directly.

The police tracking the car told Mrs. Parker they were using unmarked patrol cars to follow Meredith's abductor so as not to alert him. They had the car in sight, but no license plate was visible as of yet. A couple of times they thought they lost contact with the car, but Mrs. Parker felt that must have been when Meredith turned her phone, and therefore the GPS, off to save the batteries. Once the phone was back on, the police quickly picked up the location and were able to get back on the kidnapper's tail.

Suddenly the car went off the main road and made a turn to the right on a narrow unmarked dirt road. The police felt it was a definite path to his final destination.

They slowed but did not make the turn for fear the abductor might have a gun and get to Meredith before they could apprehend him. However, they would be forced to make the turn within a few minutes for fear of losing sight of the car. Helicopters were also waiting a couple of miles away to chase the man in case he made a run through the desert.

All of a sudden, the police reported they saw what looked like an old run-down shack through the high-powered binoculars they were using and watched as the car pulled to a stop. They held back.

Meredith felt the car bumping along, sudden slowing, and then the final stop.

She reached for her cell phone and turned it on.

Paul sat, afraid to breathe for fear she would hear him.

Mrs. Parker spoke to her. "Keep the phone on and speak as clear as you can. Don't fall apart now Meredith. We are right behind you and you will be safe." Even if the cell batteries died Mrs. Parker knew they were on track to save her. She didn't want Meredith to panic if she discovered the phone had gone dead. Both Paul and Mrs. Parker heard the trunk open.

Meredith rolled to her side and prayed. When the trunk opened, someone reached for her with rough hands. "Come on old lady, wake up. Let's get you out of the trunk."

She rolled over with the cell phone back in her pocket and squinted through the bright sunshine at the face of her abductor. In a moment of terror, she recognized the person smiling smugly down at her. She couldn't believe it! Jeffery Sanders. "What are you doing to me, Jeff?" she stammered.

He looked at her with such contempt and answered, "Getting even."

"Why, Jeff? Why would you do something like this? We all loved you."

"No, you used me," he answered. "It's time to pay back your entire family. Now they can suffer like I have all these years. Jen will lose her precious mother."

He reached for her and yanked her out of the

255

trunk. She could barely stand up. She staggered and fell against the car. He grabbed her arm forcibly and propelled her toward the cabin, so focused on his revenge he didn't even take time to look around. If he had, he might have seen the dust of the police cars in the distance headed in his direction.

He shoved open the door of the shack and pushed her down on a rickety chair in the center of the room. "Give me your hands, old lady." She felt tears begin to run down her cheeks as he grabbed her hands and tied her arms to the side of the chair.

"Please Jeff, think about what you are doing. We can talk about this."

"We are done talking," as he pulled out a knife and pressed a button to expose the blade. "Do you have any idea how long I have been following you? And you never noticed me. Just like during that sham of a marriage I was stuck in with your oh-so-darling Jennifer. No one paid any attention to me then either. I wasn't good enough for her."

Seeing the knife, Meredith froze in fear. "Oh my God, please—no. Don't hurt me."

Waving the knife in front of her face, he toyed with her, reveling in her fear. Skimming the tip down her cheek to her neck he pressed the blade into her skin, fascinated by the trail of blood now trickling from the slight cut. Moving the point down the side of her arm, Jeffery pressed the blade even deeper and dragged it down almost to her elbow. Meredith screamed as Jeff's eyes gleamed, knowing the terror and pain he was causing.

"Where should the next cut be?" he sneered.

Crying uncontrollably, Meredith shrieked, "You

will go to jail. Is that where you want to spend the rest of your life?"

He reached for a roll of duct tape. "I've had enough of your screeches," he said as he secured her mouth shut. "You and your fancy daughter are going to suffer. Your grave is already dug and I can hardly wait to drop your dead body in it."

Pacing in frustration, Paul reached for his gun as he heard Jeffery's taunts and Meredith's cries. If he was there, he would kill this man with his bare hands.

At that instant, the phone went dead. He lost communication. Mrs. Parker lost communication. Had the crazed man found her cell phone? Had he killed Meredith when he did?

Mrs. Parker stayed in touch with the police who were ready to charge the cabin. Soon it would be dark and they could move in undetected. But what if the man killed her before they got to the cabin? After a conference call between Mrs. Parker, Paul, air and land efforts, and the agency, a decision was made not to wait. Paul advised them to call out and announce their presence, offer the kidnapper freedom in return for Meredith's life, and see whether he went for it.

Just then Paul heard a commotion at the site and was told by a police commander the man had come outside to retrieve something from his car. That was all the police needed.

"Freeze!" shouted the police. Jeff Sanders reached inside the car and gunfire erupted. Paul froze, praying Meredith was safe and he was quickly reassured by a police officer she was still in the cabin.

But was she alive?

The police rushed the cabin and found Meredith

tied and gagged. It appeared her only injuries were from gashes in her neck and arm. She was quickly untied, picked up by a strong police officer, and rushed from the shack.

It all happened so fast she didn't get but a glance at the body lying in a pool of blood near the car. All she could think of was that poor mixed-up boy. God help him. How could anyone hate her family enough to want to kill her?

Paul was three hours closer to the scene. Now that he knew Meredith was safe, he had to call Jennifer and Stan. Meredith would need them to be with her as soon as possible. Before making that call, however, he asked Mrs. Parker to arrange for the local police to pick them up and take them to the Palm Springs airport where a private plane would be waiting to deliver them to wherever Meredith was being taken.

Jennifer and Stan were shocked by the news of her mother's kidnapping. The plane was waiting for them and, in their haste, they never thought to ask how all these arrangements came together so quickly. They simply did as Paul instructed and boarded the small private jet and were flown to the Marine Corp Air Base near Yuma where they were then taken to the base commander's office. All they had been told was Paul was on his way, and the police and local sheriffs were working as fast as possible to save Meredith.

Sirens blaring, the ambulance raced Meredith to the base hospital as the EMTs worked to stop the bleeding of the cuts.

When they stopped and opened the rear door, there stood Jennifer and Stan. Even as the paramedics tried to keep her out, Jennifer pushed past them to her mother and fell into her arms sobbing.

"I'm all right, Jen. Let these people do their job."

The paramedics pulled Meredith's stretcher from the ambulance while Jen rushed ahead. A doctor was waiting to suture and bandage the cuts on her injured neck and arm. Only a butterfly bandage was needed to close the cut on her neck, but the one on her arm was deep and long, requiring multiple stitches. Once they were taken care of, the doctor gave Meredith a sedative to help her rest.

Jen pulled a chair up beside her and took her hand. "Why would he do such a thing to you? Why not me? Oh, Mother, I am so sorry. He was so jealous of you and your happiness, but he will never hurt anyone again. You're safe. Paul is on his way and a lady named Mrs. Parker thinks you are the bravest woman alive. Who is she and what is this all about? Why are we on this airbase with all this special security?"

"I think Paul will explain things when he arrives but for now, I need to rest. Whatever they gave me is working. I can hardly keep my eyes open."

Her mind was swirling. Jeffery Sanders! She still couldn't believe it. She had loved him as if he was her son and he had tried to kill her. His hatred of her family had become an obsession and now he was dead. Do you ever know the real person or is everyone living lies, she wondered as her eyes closed.

Sometime later Meredith woke, still a bit drowsy. She knew Paul would somehow make everything right, but where was he and why were there soldiers all around?

Her eyes were almost closed again when suddenly the door burst open with a sound that shattered the room and like John Wayne, there stood Paul.

His eyes went directly to Meredith and she couldn't move. He walked to her, knelt, took both her hands. As the tears fell down his cheek Meredith leaned up, kissed him and the entire room fell away in silence. She encircled his head with her arms.

"Paul, none of this is your fault," Meredith whispered.

"I wasn't here to protect you, my darling."

She kissed his cheek and looked deep into his misty eyes. He stared at her in amazement. With a smile in her voice, she added, "You also need to give Mrs. Parker a raise. I could not have gotten through this ordeal without her. Do you think she could be invited to our wedding?"

Surprised, he looked into her eyes and told her how proud he was of her and how much he loved her. With a huge smile, he was quick to add, "Of course, my love."

Just then a uniformed soldier entered the room. "Mr. Richardson, please let me know if we can be of any further service to you or your staff. We will stand down now and wait for your instruction, Sir."

Confused, Meredith looked at Paul and asked, "Why is the military taking orders from you? It's time to come clean, Mr. Richardson."

"I have been trying to decide how to tell you

about my other life and guess now is as good a time as any."

He stood, walked to the window, and began explaining what he could of his double life to Meredith. Yes, he owned a very successful construction company, but in addition to the building contracts he had with multiple agencies, for the past twenty-plus years, he had also handled assignments for the United States Government.

Meredith was stunned. "Why didn't you tell me you worked for the government? So does Stephen."

"Yes, I know. Stephen has worked with me for almost nine years. But, I have only known he was your son since I received the background check I had run on you after our chance meeting at the dinner party in DC." He saw the shocked look on her face.

"Why would you investigate me?" she was quick to ask.

"That was required because of my security level. Stephen is waiting outside my office right now for a job interview. Once the interview is over, I will have him briefed and brought here as soon as I can get him on a flight."

"Paul, I can't believe all this. My son works with you?"

"He does and if I have my way he will be appointed the new department head, as I plan to retire and marry his mother. The majority of my government work is top-secret, which I am not allowed to share. The most important thing I can tell you is I love you and will be honored to have you as my wife."

Meredith stood with Paul's help and as he put his

arm around her said, "Let's go home, Paul."

Paul suggested they drop Jen and Stan off in Palm Springs on the way to Coronado. They all boarded the RCC jet that had brought Paul to the airbase and settled in for their short flight to the desert.

Jen was thrilled to learn that Stephen would be boarding the first plane from DC and meeting them in the desert after his interview at the State Department. They would be together as a family again and had so much to catch up on. Meredith also knew she had a lot of explaining to do to Claire and Heather Ann. They were aware she had been seeing someone but had no idea how serious it had become. Claire also knew nothing of the life-threatening incidents of these past weeks.

The four said their goodbyes at the door of the plane. Jen kissed her mother and Paul said they would be contacted by police regarding Jeff Sanders. They had no idea where the body had been taken and didn't care. There would be time to talk about that when their world stopped spinning.

Following take-off, Paul and Meredith sat alone in the salon. "I think you need to rest, Sunshine, and I could use a nap myself. I have had little sleep since your abduction and listening to you in that trunk almost broke my heart."

Paul reached for her hand and they walked to their bedroom. Wary of her bandaged arm, he helped remove her jacket, and she sat on the bed. "Don't worry, I will be fine, and with you at my side, I can get through anything." She lay down and Paul came to lie beside her and held her in his strong arms.

"I plan to retire from the State Department as soon as I return to Washington. Does Stephen know about me?"

"Yes, just yesterday I told him I had met someone. I mentioned your name and he didn't act as if he had ever heard it before. He must be a very good agent to not show any surprise at that type of news. But now I need to sleep; whatever medication the doctor gave me at the base is making me drowsy again." Paul's eyes looked tired too, but before she drifted off she managed to say, "There's so much I need to learn about you, my love." In what seemed like a few seconds they were asleep in each other's arms.

EPILOGUE

A few days after Meredith's successful rescue from Jeffery, Paul formalized his retirement from the government, a prime reason for celebration as they began preparing for the upcoming holidays. He was looking forward to no longer keeping secrets from his family, something now delegated to Stephen who had accepted the promotion to DC when it was offered.

Even with the end of his government career in sight, Paul knew he would be spending the majority of his final three weeks in DC helping to bring Stephen up to date. Although he couldn't wait to be in Coronado with Meredith full time, he knew how important it was to give Stephen the right start. The luxury of owning a private plane meant either Meredith was with him in Washington or he spent weekends with her in California during those weeks.

On the final day of his secret government life, Paul felt as if Santa had delivered a major Christmas gift early. He was officially retired.

Upon leaving DC, Paul moved into Meredith's condo and they spent all of their evenings together, which made him feel he had a true home for the first time in years. After juggling two high-profile jobs, and flying all over the globe for the majority of his life, he spent only a few hours a week at the newest branch of RCC now established in his downtown San Diego hotel. The only major iron he had in the works was helping Meredith plan for their wedding the third week of January and that didn't take much time as he had the right people in place in Hawaii to handle the preparations.

Although Meredith loved having him with her full time, she often accused him of invading her space and jokingly told him, "If you don't stay on your side of the condo so I stop tripping over you, I may move you to the patio." He needed a project and seeing that this condo was simply too small for them, decided he would find them a larger unit.

Paul didn't feel his home in Hawaii should be considered their primary residence. They needed a place on the mainland. The Shores was the perfect spot for travels in and out of the area. Amenities were endless, security was provided, and they could safely lock the door and leave anytime they desired.

The next day, he sat reading the Coronado Journal newspaper and glanced through the many listings of properties for sale. He knew they had to be on the ocean side and if he was lucky enough to find a large three-bedroom on a corner similar to Meredith's current location, he would snatch it up as another surprise for her. His dilemma was would she want to move.

Telling her he was off to the office, he met with a realtor and studied the open listings. A couple of them caught his eye but realizing a change of this size must be a joint decision, he arranged for a showing later in the week, after he presented his idea to Meredith. He could hardly wait to tell her about his latest project. Who knows, she might suggest he could live there alone, but he would take his chances.

After dinner and a glass of wine on the patio, he brought up the subject of their condo. "This place is adequate for one but it's a bit crowded for the two of us. I think we need more space." He could see her studying him and knew she had already figured out he was up to something.

"Paul, are you suggesting a move?"

"What do you think about the idea?" he asked.

"I think a larger place is a splendid idea. I'm guessing you have already started the search, so let's hear your plans."

When he told her he had met with a realtor she wasn't surprised. "There are a limited number of larger units available," he said. "Will you go with me one day during the week to view them?"

"Of course," she exclaimed, getting very excited. A new home and a wedding!

The following Wednesday they met the realtor and toured the available listings. The first unit they saw was in El Bonita Tower and had a wonderful corner view of both the city and ocean but it overlooked the small public parking area for the beachgoers, so it dropped to the bottom of their list. The next unit in El Conquistador directly faced the ocean, something Meredith was not too excited about. She did appreciate its size, much larger than the first one, but pointed out it needed a complete remodel, head to toe. The third unit was in the appropriately named La Paraiso building, had a great corner view of both ocean and city, was completely remodeled, move-in ready, and of course, came with a very hefty price tag.

They thanked the realtor and as they walked back to their condo, Paul took her hand and pulled her to a stop. Looking deep into her eyes he asked, "Which one do you want?" She couldn't believe his words. Just like that—which one did she want? Was it that easy for him to buy and sell things?

She said in her most dramatic Scarlett O'Hara voice, "I will think about that tomorrow Mr. Richardson. First, it's time for dinner."

That night after a wonderful evening of lovemaking, she laid encircled in his arms. She thought he was asleep as she whispered, "La Paraiso."

He opened one eye and stared down at her. "What a way to get a new home. And yes, you can have La Paraiso since you are my true paradise. We'll start negotiations in the morning. Good night my love." Excitement soared within her and she could not wait to call her daughters with the news.

The next morning, after the exciting phone call from Meredith, Jennifer thought about how wonderful life had become for her mother. She and Paul would start their married life in a new home creating new memories. Although Dad would always be with them, it was time for Mother to begin a new life with Paul.

Claire was also happy for her mother. Although she had not met Paul in person, her mother had mentioned him during numerous phone calls. Her siblings had shared their positive thoughts about him, so Claire was sure she would like him as well.

Stephen was currently living in guest quarters in DC. He spent the days with the staff learning the ropes of his new position and Paul joined the briefings whenever required. Although his family was not moving back to the States with him initially, he hoped he and Loren would be able to work out their differences soon so they would all be together. Unfortunately, this new role meant even tighter security and more secrets.

The more time he spent with Paul, the more comfortable Stephen became with his mother's choice. Paul was very different from his father, but they were also alike in many ways. They were both driven and successful in their professional lives, both were large men who towered over his petite mom, and both loved her unconditionally.

Meredith was overwhelmed with how quickly the purchase of the new condo occurred. Paul hired the best moving company available so she was able to stand back and supervise. Getting settled after such a big move, even the short distance across the parking lot, was a daunting task. Paul brought some of his hotel staff to help get them unpacked and settled. No major arguments occurred between them, which Meredith thought was a miracle.

They talked about what to do with Meredith's

condo in the El Cortez building and decided to title it over to Jennifer as her Christmas gift. It was to be kept in her name and at her discretion could be loaned to family members wanting to visit the beach. The one provision was that she should keep it in the family, which Meredith knew she would.

Thanksgiving would be the perfect time to bring both families together and Paul had the ideal place—his private hotel in San Diego. It was near Jennifer and Stan, and he would fly his boys and their spouses to San Diego for the long weekend. Stephen's family would be traveling the farthest, and Claire might need the most advance notice due to possible court cases, but he was sure they could all arrange their busy schedules for the holiday celebration. He also wanted to include Jake, his best friend who, with no family of his own, was always at his side.

He asked his private chef to prepare the feast and planned to use the larger hotel dining room which would provide plenty of room for all. Everyone could relax and hopefully get to know one another, and best of all, no one in the family would have to cook or do the dishes.

He made all the travel arrangements himself and surprised Meredith with the details. She was thrilled and Paul smiled to himself, realizing he had just planned the first family event in his entire life. Meredith took over the seating plans, careful to intersperse her family with Paul's sons and their wives so the soon-to-be blended families could get acquainted. She put the younger children together and seated Claire and Jake next to each other hoping for a spark to ignite between them.

Thanksgiving dinner was an all-day event. The meal was extraordinary and beautifully served. Instead of flowers, the turkey sat in its place of honor in the center of the large oval table surrounded by all the traditional trimmings.

Meredith tried not to pay too much attention to Jake and Claire during dinner but noticed they disappeared after dessert was served. She asked Paul, "Do you know where Claire and Jake have gone?"

"No, but given your matchmaking, I'm guessing they might have wanted some time alone." Meredith tried to look shocked until Paul leaned over to kiss her on the cheek. "Good job." When the couple re-entered the room, the smiles on their faces gave Meredith hope.

Paul had arranged for a small combo to provide background music for the evening. Taking Meredith's hand, he led her to the dance floor, inviting everyone to join them. Looking around the floor, now crowded with their families, she noticed Jake and Claire dancing close together. Maybe her hunch was paying off.

Hours later, all of the family members were laughing, sharing stories, and looking forward to seeing each other again. As the evening was winding down, Paul asked everyone to make plans to be with them over the Christmas holidays, a suggestion greeted with resounding applause.

After the excitement of Thanksgiving, Paul felt the need for a short break and he asked her over their morning coffee, "How does a quick trip to Vancouver sound? You have friends there to visit and, even if it's a bit chilly, I can keep you warm in my arms. Plus, I know you have two drawers full of socks," he teased.

Meredith was elated, both to see her old friends and to *get out of Dodge*. The wedding was all arranged, so why not take off on a whim for a few days. She had gone from being the world's great planner to the spontaneity queen of Coronado, easy to do when you have a private airplane at your disposal, so off they went.

When they returned home, the couple began thinking about Christmas, Meredith's favorite holiday. In preparation for their first yuletide season together, and in between short trips to his office, Paul began making arrangements for the family visits. He decided he liked planning for their families and *party planner* became his newest title.

He was winding down his day-to-day operations as CEO of his company, passing more and more control to his sons. Paul Junior privately confided he and his wife, Alison, were trying hard to adopt a child and Paul hoped they would surprise him with the title of Grandpa by Christmas.

Their families seemed to be tracking their every move. The phone rang constantly with either his children or hers. They had become the center of attention and loved every minute of it.

They decorated the tree together while enjoying eggnog and brandy and, exhausted, fell into bed wrapped in each other's arms. Ten days later, the family began descending on the new Coronado condo. It was wonderful to see everyone again so soon after Thanksgiving. It was becoming very convenient to use Paul's private hotel in the city as party central.

Once again, the entire family was seated around the large table for a feast, followed by the oh's, ah's, and thank you's as Christmas gifts under the spectacular tree were opened.

Meredith was overwhelmed when she opened a large box, her gift from Paul, to find his college letterman jacket inside with a card that read, "It's about time you had this. Along with all my love." As he helped her try it on, he whispered in her ear, "Check the pockets."

When she did, Meredith found a yellow diamond solitaire engagement ring. Smiling down at her, Paul said, "I thought it was time for you to have one of those as well." And, with a kiss, he placed it on the ring finger of her left hand.

Her gift to him was simple. She said, "Yes!" and all of the family cheered.

The wedding three weeks later was held on the beach of the Hilton Hawaiian Village. Seeing the tears in the eyes of the loving couple erased any doubts their children might have had about their perfect union.

Paul had flown both families to Hawaii for the

ceremony. All five of their children and their spouses or significant others and Meredith's three grandchildren were excited to be in attendance.

His real surprise for Meredith was a brief visit from Dr. Karen, her dearest friend. She was able to join them for the ceremony but had to leave soon afterward to return to State Department headquarters. She had brought the two of them together in DC and he was glad she could break away from her busy schedule even for a few hours to come to the wedding of her two dear friends.

When Stephen heard Karen was able to come, he asked her to represent the family and walk Meredith down the makeshift aisle in the sand to the water's edge to become Mrs. Paul Richardson. Karen felt honored to be given the task and when she arrived in the early afternoon the tears of surprise and joy on Meredith's face made Paul's heart almost leap out of his chest. He had pulled off one more great surprise.

Looking over the small group of friends and family gathered, he felt for the first time in many years the true meaning of family. He promised himself to make sure they all remained close and safe for the rest of their lives.

All of the wedding attendees were dressed in Hawaiian attire. Meredith wore a long white cotton lace dress chosen with the help of her daughters, and everyone was dressed casually except Paul, who chose to add a sports jacket over his Hawaiian shirt. Sandals adorned almost everyone's feet, as is the custom for a beach wedding; Paul chose topsiders. She would have to work on a more casual wardrobe for him as he converted to a beach lifestyle, but she had a lifetime to try.

The wedding ceremony began with messages from all five of their children congratulating the two who had unexpectedly found each other, and love again, after such a long time apart.

Meredith had planned her own surprise for Paul. As they stood at the makeshift altar in the sand, she took Paul's hand in hers and as she placed a platinum band on the ring finger of his left hand, began reciting lines from her favorite song. To Meredith, the song signified her life with Alex and now Paul, her two extraordinary loves. As she spoke the crowd stilled.

"What are you doing the rest of your life?
I have only one request of your life,
That you spend it all with me.
In the world of love you keep in your eyes,
What I will recall of my life,
Is all of my new life with you."

There wasn't a dry eye in the group and even the Hawaiian minister who officiated cleared his throat before he could announce them as Mr. and Mrs. Paul Richardson. It was the perfect ending to their beautiful beach wedding.

A luau reception followed the ceremony. A long table was set up directly on the beach with beautiful flowers and elegant table settings just as Meredith would have designed herself. Soft Hawaiian music was played by local musicians and everyone danced. Paul danced with Mrs. Parker and Jake shared a dance with Meredith. Young Derrick, now almost five feet tall, danced with Karen and Heather Ann, while Loren and Samantha did a hula of sorts.

Meredith noticed Jake held Claire in his arms again as he had at Thanksgiving. Once she and Paul returned from their honeymoon, she promised to give the pairing a little extra nudge. She also saw the way Stephen held Loren and hoped in her heart there was romance coming back into their lives.

The fire pit gave a warm glow to the evening and a beautiful wedding cake was presented to the bride and groom carried in by her three grandchildren. Gorgeous weather, a glowing fire, the beach beyond, and every heart in attendance was overwhelmed. The setting was as perfect as their parent's love for each other.

After a very long day and evening, Meredith said goodbye to Karen and thanked her for taking the time to come so far to attend their big event. The small group disbanded and sent the bride and groom off to their suite to begin their long-awaited honeymoon. Little did their children know the honeymoon had started that wonderful night almost three months ago in their friendly skies.

They were married at last. How could life be so perfect the second time around?

Meredith and Paul rode the tower elevator to their suite and couldn't resist their usual long lingering kiss in their own private space. Paul made a mental note to surprise the grandchildren with a large amount of stock in Otis Elevator next Christmas and hoped they would each use it as wisely as their grandparents had.

After a tender night of lovemaking, they slept in

the contentment of each other's arms. The next morning the entire family shared breakfast in their suite. The family was curious about the surprise Paul had planned for Meredith. They all tried to trick him into telling them where he was taking her for their honeymoon but he held fast. "I've had years of practice keeping secrets—there is no breaking me now," he joked.

Paul wanted to surprise Meredith and would not tell her anything except it was a place guaranteed to be paradise on earth.

"This is my last secret, let me enjoy it."

Meredith packed, kissed everyone a tearful goodbye, and set out with Paul for the airport not knowing where they were going. She had laughingly suggested they all come along, but Paul was quick to say this was their time alone and at their age, they didn't need a family of chaperones.

Jake drove them to the airport, and they sat quietly holding hands in the back seat. Meredith was dying to ask him where this mysterious place was but played along with his big surprise.

They arrived at the airport and once they stepped from the car Paul shook Jake's hand and wished him a wonderful, well-deserved vacation. Meredith suddenly realized they were at the public airport terminal and she leaned in to give Jake a quick kiss on the cheek, also wishing him a relaxing vacation.

For the first time since she had lunch with Paul in Washington, they were completely alone. No private jet and crew. No private driver. They were two lovers going on their honeymoon. They boarded the plane in first class and were ushered to their seats. Meredith thought for sure Paul had bought out the entire section as the rear of the plane was crowded while they sat alone in first class.

Once they were settled and ready for takeoff the stewardess brought two glasses of their favorite champagne and they toasted to their new life together.

The destination at the gate was Maui so at least she now knew where they were heading and it was only a short forty-five-minute flight.

When the plane landed at the Lihue side of the Island, Paul walked her over to the rental car counter. "No frills on this honeymoon," he said. He was trying hard to be the ordinary tourist, one identity he hadn't held in years, but when a silver four-door Jaguar was pulled up, she realized no one would ever accuse him of being ordinary.

Sitting next to Paul was the most comfortable place she could imagine. He didn't even mind her fussing over him, as her entire family had warned him she would do. He just laughed and took it in stride.

She had decided not to question where they were going. She would rather go along with the gleam in his eyes, as she had done so often with Alex. Meredith no longer compared the two men in her life but cherished the love from both.

They drove about fifteen minutes to an unmarked road where the sign read *private*. What would be at the end of the road?

It was as if they were driving toward the river's edge but this time they were married and free to express all their feelings and love for each other.

Paul rounded the bend and approached a small house that looked like a Hawaiian painting. As they neared, the house seemed to grow larger and Meredith began to see the sprawling roofline. She thought it might be a small hotel. The long, secluded driveway led towards the porte cochère at the front entrance. After stopping the car, Paul quickly came around to open the car door for Meredith. She was again reminded of the river's edge, only this time she graciously accepted his hand, the same hand she had refused over forty years ago.

Hand in hand they walked through the large etched glass doors.

"Welcome to your new home, Mrs. Richardson," he said with a smile in his voice. The sight was breathtaking. Meredith heard her beloved jagged waves and began to cry. Paul took her in his arms and held her close. All she could manage to say between sobs was how much she loved him.

"I can't believe this beautiful place will be our home."

"This has been my private hideaway for years and no one, not even Jake, has been here." He walked her through the open spaces to the patio and they both stood staring at the water.

"You always said you wanted to sleep outdoors." Turning, she noticed a bed sitting at the patio's edge overlooking the blue Pacific, strewn with yellow rose petals.

Meredith looked back to Paul. Taking his face in her hands she said, "Can we live here forever?"

"Of course, my darling. I thought often about you sharing your life with me here. And my dreams have finally come true. I love you so, Mrs. Richardson."

"And I love you too. This truly is Paradise."

ABOUT THE AUTHOR

Jillian Night started her career as a newspaper writer in Orange County, California. *Jagged Waves* is her first novel. Herself a widow, Jillian lives quietly in Palm Springs surrounded by her many friends and family who encouraged her to write this story of a love long-forgotten.

She is especially thankful to her editor, Betsi Newbury, who keeps her on the right track and is her true right and left arm.

Enjoy a sneak peek of

SHATTERED DREAMS

CHAPTER 1

J agged waves had once again changed the life of Meredith Jamison Richardson. New waves across the Pacific were now hers to enjoy and she was living an enchanted life married to her old college beau and deeply in love with Paul Richardson.

Their wedding had taken place ten days earlier at their favorite hotel in Honolulu, The Hilton Hawaiian Village, and signaled more than the blending of their two families. It was the culmination of Paul's lifelong dream to have Meredith at his side, this time as his wife.

Following their wedding ceremony, they boarded a commercial flight to the Luhie side of the island of Maui for their honeymoon. Eager to introduce his bride to his exclusive hideaway and their new home, he kept their destination a secret from Meredith. As they drove down the narrow road, she felt as if they were going back in time forty years to their private riverbank in Phoenix. When they rounded the last bend she was awed by the beautiful home and grounds.

Walking through the etched-glass doors into the large open entryway, Meredith was stunned by the panoramic view of the Pacific ocean a few yards away. As they roamed through the impressive living space, Meredith and Paul noticed a huge floral bouquet and an iced bottle of champagne. The attached congratulatory note to the newlyweds was signed by Sheila and James Makua, the Hawaiian couple who served as house managers. Paul wasted no time opening the Dom Perignon, offering a glass to Meredith. After a lingering kiss, Paul said, "Go and enjoy your new ocean waves. I will refill our glasses and meet you on the patio in a few minutes."

The home was designed by renowned Hawaiian architect Olson Kandi who happened to be an old friend from Paul's time spent in government service, and who had gone from designing buildings to beautiful Hawaiian-style homes. Most all rooms were open to the elements, which concerned Meredith as the islands were always at risk of serious storms, but Paul showed her the many secret pocket doors with sturdy latches, and she soon realized he had thought of everything to keep them safe and secure.

The next morning, away from the city noises they were accustomed to, Paul rolled over and took Meredith in his arms, gently making love to her as they enjoyed the soft silence of the waves lapping on the shore and the beating of their hearts.

They soon settled into a light routine of mostly doing nothing. They walked what seemed like miles, just holding hands and enjoying their surroundings. Meals were simple and served a few steps outside on their patio with a view only God could have created.

It took a couple of weeks for Meredith to get used to her new environment. The peaceful island was very quiet in comparison to the lively San Diego lifestyle she was accustomed to. Even learning their way around the small island town and locating the grocery store, which was no longer on the corner, was a challenge. With their families on the mainland, life became just the two of them.

She rearranged the furniture, just slightly so Paul wouldn't notice, which of course he did, but let her have her way as with everything these days. He spoiled her rotten and, in turn, she became his "beck and call girl."

Meredith quickly realized she had left her cooking skills in San Diego but Paul never complained. He was quick to remind her, "there is always Gin and Tonic." He became the Barbecuer-in-Chief, but when Meredith burned her favorite macaroni and cheese he felt it was time for an intervention and offered his help in the kitchen. Soon, all of the slicing, dicing, and chopping Meredith had him doing gave him new respect for his private chef, Gerrard, now on vacation somewhere in Europe. Cooking side by side, and even the burned mac and cheese, made life for the romantic duo a special event.

While Paul often reflected on the wasted years before unexpectedly meeting Meredith again at a DC state dinner, he knew he never would have become the man he was now without those life lessons. His wife Rachel's tragic drowning after years of alcoholism and his years of working secretly for the United States Government had left him with many sleepless nights. He often worried about the strain that put on his relationships with his sons.

Even though David and Paul Junior had helped him build Richardson Construction Company to its current stature, there were times he felt closer to Meredith's son Stephen now heading Paul's old government team in Washington. "I guess secrets kept, danger, and intrigue build stronger relationships," he thought to himself as he shook off the pensive mood and went in search of his Meredith.

A few days later Paul suggested they drive to Kaanapali and enjoy some of his favorite island restaurants, namely Fleetwood's and The Lahaina Grill. Meredith was thrilled with his idea and within thirty minutes Paul booked an oceanfront suite at the Hyatt Regency and their honeymoon began all over again. The couple greatly appreciated the hotel's room service, and the aroma of the Kona coffee served them each morning was almost as good as Jake's... well almost.

On the third morning of their second honeymoon, Paul suggested a round of golf at Kapahulu and asked Meredith to join him. "I would love to be your caddy," she was proud to announce. Paul knew this was a big step, considering the way her husband had died so suddenly on the Coronado Golf Course. He could sense her deep in thought as he stepped on the first tee, but soon a smile returned to her face and she was once again his.

The weather was golf perfect and they both laughed at just how bad a duffer he was. Meredith lost count of the many balls that landed in the ocean. He had never taken time to become a real golfer, but with Meredith at his side, knew the game could become one of his favorite new hobbies. He would encourage her to take lessons when they got back home to Coronado.

As they drove back to the Lihue side of the island Paul brought up the idea of going home for a few days to touch base with their children and of course, RCC, which Meredith knew still tugged at his heartstrings. She eagerly agreed, for as much as she loved their Hawaiian home, she was beginning to miss the hustle and bustle of Coronado.

Although he rarely spoke of it, Meredith felt that Paul missed his sons. One of her deepest desires became finding a way to bring all of them together again. She hoped the hurt they felt was not too deep to overcome and knew that her plans to bring them closer would be much easier to put into motion on the mainland.

Their trip home a few days later was on the company jet with Jake Skyler once again at the controls. Meredith was so pleased to see Jake she flung her arms around him and kissed his cheek. He blushed and acted a bit shy at her show of affection and it made her wonder if he had or ever could love anyone.

Meredith's daughter Jennifer, and her partner Stan Barrington, greeted them at San Diego's executive terminal and drove them to their condo at The Shores. When they entered their unit at the Paraiso Tower, it truly felt like home. The table was set and Jen had dinner in the oven, Paul's favorite meatloaf, and the four of them talked and laughed through the meal. They were finally a real family.

Later that evening when she entered their bedroom Meredith could not hold back the uncontrollable tears that ran down her cheeks and she reached for Paul. Her life had come full circle, all due to this wonderful man now holding her in his arms.

The next morning Paul was off to his make-shift

289

office in the hotel owned by RCC just ten minutes over the bridge in the Gaslamp District of the city. He couldn't quite get a grip on retirement, although he tried.

Truth be told, Meredith was glad to have a little time to herself so she could start putting some of her motherly   schemes   into   motion.

Made in the USA
Middletown, DE
24 September 2022

10796062R10172